𝕷𝖎𝖓𝖈𝖔𝖑𝖓 𝕻𝖚𝖇𝖑𝖎𝖈 𝕷𝖎𝖇𝖗𝖆𝖗𝖞

September 1980

THE
GRANDMOTHER

THE
GRANDMOTHER

Georges Simenon

Translated by Jean Stewart

A Helen and Kurt Wolff Book

Harcourt Brace Jovanovich
New York and London

September 1980

Library of Congress Cataloging in Publication Data

Simenon, Georges, 1903–
The grandmother.
Translation of La Vieille.
"A Helen and Kurt Wolff book."
I. Title.
PZ3.S5892Gr [PQ2637.I53] 843'.912 80-14918
ISBN 0-15-136738-8

Printed in the United States of America

First American edition

B C D E

ONE

Under an archway as cold and dank as a cellar, the Police Superintendent paused for a moment, looked at his wrist watch and shook his coat, scattering drops of melted snow on the sidewalk, where they spread as though on blotting paper. It was five minutes past eleven.

When he had paid his earlier visit, at half past nine that morning, the concierge, a young, rather pretty woman living in a comfortable porter's lodge, had been unimpressed by his title or by his courteous manner, and had answered him rather crossly.

"You haven't come to arrest the lady, I trust."

"Nothing of the sort, of course."

"If it's because her car's been picked up again, Lord knows where . . ."

"Not at all. This isn't even an official visit, strictly speaking. It happens that Mademoiselle Emel may be able to provide me with some information, and even possibly to help me."

Without interrupting the buzz of her vacuum cleaner, the concierge cast an ironic glance at him.

"If you want her help, I'd advise you not to bother her at this time of day. She never gets up before eleven, and more likely at two or three in the afternoon."

This was his second visit, then, and before going any farther he removed his hat to shake off the big drops of murky water that covered it, replaced it on his head, and stamped with his right foot and then with his left to get rid of the melting snow, so that a great wet patch now lay on the sidewalk. Through the glass door the concierge, in her black dress and white apron, watched him with indifference, neither encouraging nor discouraging him.

A staircase rose to the left of the archway and another to the right, each with a wrought-iron railing ending in a brass knob. Beyond, on the other side of the courtyard, where a flight of steps led up to the door of an old mansion, a few patches of snow still lay between the round cobblestones.

Not knowing which way to go, the Superintendent retraced his steps, and the concierge, who had been watching him, opened the door a crack to inform him, condescendingly:

"Left-hand staircase. Fifth floor."

He did not ask whether there was an elevator; that was unlikely. The old houses of the Ile Saint-Louis, most of which are of historic interest, are ill adapted to such unwieldy contraptions, the mere suggestion of which would shock certain house owners.

He started slowly up the stairs, hearing no sound behind any of the carved doors, and only on the third floor did he seek the support of the railing. On the fifth floor he stopped to recover his breath before pressing the electric bell, and waited motionless for what seemed a long time. He consulted his watch again. He was wondering whether to ring a second time when he detected a shuffling sound; then there was a pause, and finally the click of a well-oiled lock.

The door opened barely a few inches. A maid dressed in black and white like the concierge, short and sturdy, was looking at him silently in much the same way as the woman down below, as though there were something incongruous about his appearance. In fact, the Superintendent was correctly, even elegantly, dressed, and could not have been mistaken for a summons server or a salesman of vacuum cleaners or encyclopedias.

"Is Mademoiselle Emel at home?" he asked quietly, holding out a calling card, which he had extracted from his wallet while climbing the stairs.

His hands were wet from touching his coat; having only had a short way to come, he had not thought it necessary to take his car.

"I'll go and see."

The maid seemed on the point of closing the door, but shrugged her shoulders and moved away without either shutting it or opening it wider.

At the far end of the apartment he heard women's voices, followed by hurried comings and goings, as though things were hastily being tidied up. Then, nearer by, a voice asked distinctly:

"Where is he?"

"I left him on the landing."

The oak door opened wider, and the Superintendent stood face to face with Sophie Emel, who, while

3

bearing some resemblance to the photographs published in newspapers and magazines, made a very different impression on him. It was not the first time that, in the course of his duties, he had met famous people in their private surroundings. Nonetheless, he was disconcerted by the tight-fitting scarlet pants, like a bullfighter's, the bare feet on the carpet, and the turtleneck sweater that the young woman had hastily pulled on, ruffling her hair.

Holding his card, she said sleepily:

"I'm so sorry you weren't shown in."

It was obvious that she did not mean this, that she couldn't care less.

"It's I who must apologize, mademoiselle, for disturbing you."

And, as though it was really early in the morning, he added:

"At this time of day."

"Come this way."

She led him along a white-walled corridor, where, through a half-open door, he caught a glimpse of an untidy bathroom. A moment later they were in a huge room that looked like an artist's studio, the bay window of which framed the towers of Notre-Dame against a sky still heavy with snow clouds.

Another young woman was hurriedly slipping on a housecoat over her black silk pajamas. Her hair was so fair as to be almost white, her skin and eyes so pale that she looked like an albino.

"I suppose you know Lélia?"

He had heard speak of her, too, had seen her on posters and on television.

"I'm delighted."

4

Lélia, with the hoarse voice of someone who has drunk and smoked too much the night before, was saying to her friend:

"I'll leave you two together."

"Don't go away. I'm sure it's nothing secret."

High-heeled shoes lay untidily on the floor, an evening dress hung over the arm of an easy chair, and on a small table stood a bottle of whisky three-quarters empty, two glasses, and cigarette butts stained with lipstick. The bottle and glasses must have been there since the previous night, for on another table there were steaming cups of coffee beside some half-eaten croissants.

"Sit down, monsieur." Sophie Emel glanced at the card. "Monsieur Charon, isn't it?"

He felt somewhat embarrassed at seeing, right in front of him, a pearl-gray bedroom and twin beds whose covers had been thrown back and which seemed still to bear the warm imprint of bodies.

"Do you smoke?"

He accepted a cigarette in order to keep some composure while he sat on the edge of a satin-covered armchair.

"I must apologize for this visit, which is quite unofficial. The fact is that for some time I've been in an awkward fix, and I must admit that I'm counting on you a little to help me."

Sophie Emel was perched on the arm of an easy chair, her cup of coffee in one hand and a cigarette in the other.

"I suppose you don't want any coffee? You must have been up a long time."

"A fairly long time, yes . . . It was quite by chance

5

that your name came up in connection with the case that's bothering me. First of all, if I may, I'll ask you a question. Do you know somebody named Juliette Viou?"

She stared at him as though searching her memory.

"Viou, you said?"

"A woman who's now seventy-nine years old."

"Juliette Viou . . ." she repeated. "Viou . . . Viou . . ."

"Just a minute. Before becoming Juliette Viou, she was the widow of a man named Prédicant."

"Well, well!" Sophie called out to her friend, "Do you know who's turned up?"

"No."

"My grandmother."

She turned to the Superintendent, her curiosity aroused.

"Tell us! What's happened to my grandmother? You're not going to tell me she's murdered somebody!"

He felt impelled to smile.

"Nothing of the sort, of course."

"It might well happen. . . . Has she had an accident?"

"Don't worry."

"Do you know, Superintendent, how long it is since my family has had any news of her?"

Uneasy, he murmured:

"Actually, I know very little about the lady."

"She left home when we were still living on Boulevard Saint-Germain. That was . . . wait a minute . . . nearly fifteen years ago. Work it out for yourself. It

6

was in November or December 1944. I don't remember exactly, but the first winter after Paris was liberated. . . . The streets were still lit with blue lamps. . . . My grandmother was sixty-five at the time, and to me and my twin sister—we were then twelve years old— she seemed a very old woman. . . . Since you call her Juliette Viou, I assume she must have remarried."

He nodded, adding:

"She was widowed again a year and a half ago."

"Has she been living in Paris all the time?"

He nodded again, and seemed to hunt for his words.

"It's precisely in connection with her present residence . . . I mean the place she's living in . . . that I . . ."

He had always been careful to show tact in the exercise of his duties, and he had never needed it more.

"Won't you have a drink?"

"No, thanks."

"Give me a Scotch, Lélia. The coffee's disagreeing with me. Help yourself, if you want some."

She explained to the Superintendent:

"We've both got a hangover. When you rang, we were thinking of going back to bed. That was probably why we reacted so oddly when Louise told us a police superintendent was asking for me. You were saying that my grandmother . . ."

"It's rather complicated. For a good many years now she's been living in an old house on Rue de Jouy."

"Quite close to here, across the bridge?"

He went on:

"You may have seen from your windows those old houses being demolished in the Hôtel de Ville and Saint-Paul districts. It's all part of a slum-clearance scheme long overdue."

"No water, Lélia! I'll take it neat, to start with."

She swallowed the Scotch as though it were medicine, and, after a sudden spasmodic gulp, seemed more in control of herself.

"Go on."

"Madame Juliette Viou was living, first with her husband and then alone, right at the top of one of those houses. The tenants received notice to leave two years ago."

"I suppose my grandmother refused to leave."

And turning to her friend:

"Do you hear that, Lélia? I'll have to tell you about her. . . . I'm listening, Superintendent."

"The apartments were vacated one after the other. On some floors the doors and windows are gone. One of the walls, which had become dangerous to neighboring houses and to passers-by, has been shored up, after a fashion. According to orders, the building should have been pulled down eighteen months ago, and I don't know why the work was held up. The fact remains that a shoemaker who had his shop on the ground floor, looking out on the courtyard, stayed there until last month. As for your grandmother . . ."

He corrected himself:

"I mean Madame Viou . . ."

"You can call her my 'grandmother.' "

"In her case, my department discovered only three

weeks ago that she was still occupying her rooms on the top floor. I must explain that the dormer windows open above the cornice, so that from the street . . ."

"Is she still there?"

Now Sophie poured a small amount of water into her glass and lit a fresh cigarette.

"Listen to this, Lélia! I can see it's going to be fascinating."

"I was all the more surprised to find that a tenant was still living in the building, because the water, gas, and electricity were all cut off over a year ago. On orders from the Ministry of Public Works, I sent an inspector there. He went up to the fifth floor and knocked at the only door still standing. It was not until he threatened to break down that door that he heard a voice, inside:

" 'Tell your boss that I was here in 1902, before he was born, and that I will only go out feet first.' "

The Superintendent hurriedly added:

"I apologize for quoting that remark, but it reflects the obstinacy we have to deal with."

"I'm not shocked." And Sophie added, after taking another sip, "Quite the contrary!"

"The demolition work was finally supposed to begin yesterday. I got it postponed until tomorrow. During the last few weeks my inspectors have repeatedly returned to Rue de Jouy, and when, as a last resort, they brought a locksmith along with them, Madame Viou told them, still speaking behind the closed door:

" 'If you try to force an entrance, I warn you I shall jump out of the window.' "

9

"Do you hear, Lélia? And what then?"

"I'll spare you the administrative and legal details that the situation entails."

"So my grandmother, all by herself, is holding up the demolition of this building?"

"During the past two weeks, plain-clothes policemen have been taking turns hiding outside, waiting for her to come out, in order to prevent her going back into the place."

"And she's never come out?"

"She merely taunts us by throwing empty cans out of the window every day. She seems to have laid in enough to stand a siege."

"What does she do about water?"

"Unfortunately, there's been a lot of rain lately. The people in the house opposite have seen her lean out of her window each time it's rained to collect water from the cornice. She must have pails full."

"So, all in all, there's nothing you can do?"

"I'd be within my rights if I were to disregard her threats and break down the door. It's by no means certain that she would jump out the window."

"I'm pretty sure she would."

"That's what the doctor thinks, too."

"What doctor?"

"I went along myself, on two occasions, to argue with her through the door, and the second time I took a psychiatrist with me."

Sophie Emel frowned as she asked in a harsher voice:

"Do you intend to put her in an institution?"

"That's not the question, now that we know who Madame Viou is. I'd like you to try to see the situation from the administrative point of view. Until quite recently we were never concerned with her and we were practically unaware of her existence. . . . It was not until last month that we consulted our registers, and we only know what they tell us."

He drew from his pocket a piece of paper.

"Juliette Thérèse Marie-Joseph Minoré, born Moulins, Allier, 12 September 1879, married Adrien Dieudonné Viou 15 November 1901, at the town hall of Moulins . . ."

"I knew she'd had a first husband before she married my grandfather, but I was never told who he was. What did this Viou do for a living?"

"He's registered as a journalist. He and your grandmother were divorced in 1910, and in 1911 she married Gilbert Prédicant, a printer, from Paris."

"My grandfather. He died when I was four years old, and Grandmother came to live with my parents on Boulevard Saint-Germain, until she suddenly disappeared in 1944. . . ."

"Well, according to the register, she went back to her first husband, whom she married again three years later. Strange to say, Viou was still living in the apartment on Rue de Jouy where he had been registered in 1901. In 1959 we find your grandmother living there and refusing to leave the place. Since her name does not appear on the Social Security lists, we assume that she has private means. Neither she nor her husband was ever in a hospital. Even if we succeed in evicting her forcibly from that house, we cannot simply abandon her on the sidewalk.

"I'd like you to understand. We can't send her to one of the city hospitals if she isn't ill, nor would we be entitled to relocate her against her will in another apartment, even if one were available.

"Can you picture the situation? Suppose my men were to bring her down. There they would be on a crowded street with a screaming, struggling old woman on their hands. . . ."

"That's why you considered having her institutionalized?"

"At one point that seemed the only solution, because her stubborn insistence on remaining all alone in a building that might come crashing down at any moment could be taken as a sign of mental instability."

"What did the psychiatrist say?"

"He asked her questions."

"Through the door?"

"There was no alternative."

"Did she answer?"

"She's talkative. She's high-spirited, too. She made fun of him, and of me, claiming to have enough supplies for six months and kerosene for her stove. I'm worried about that kerosene in such a dilapidated house."

"Does the doctor think she's mad?"

He looked embarrassed.

"He'd be prepared, if need be, to sign an order for her to be provisionally committed and kept under observation. But now that we know she has relatives, we can do nothing without their consent."

"So you've come to ask me for my agreement?"

She was looking at him much as the concierge and the maid had.

"No. Believe me, I understand what a tricky situation this is. When I learned, quite by chance, that you might be related to Juliette Viou ..."

"Who told you?"

"It happened in the most unexpected way. One of my inspectors recently read your biography in a magazine. The article mentioned your middle-class background, pointing out that your father was a well-known publisher and your maternal grandfather the owner of the Prédicant Press. My inspector was struck by the name, which he remembered having seen, and he looked up Juliette Viou's name in the register again. . . . The merest chance . . . Right now I've got some men on the staircase of the Rue de Jouy house, others on the sidewalk and in the courtyard. . . . Tomorrow the demolition crew will be getting to work. . . . It suddenly struck me that if you were willing to talk to your grandmother ..."

"What could I say to her?"

"I don't know. It's essential that she realize ..."

"When?"

"I was hoping ..."

"Would you like me to go right away? What do you think, Lélia?"

"She's not my grandmother."

"Will you come with us?"

"I'd rather not."

Sophie Emel turned to the Superintendent.

"There are no reporters or photographers there, I hope."

"You must realize that in my situation I've no desire for publicity."

Sophie opened a door.

"Louise! Get some clothes ready for me."

"What are you going to wear, mademoiselle?"

"Oh, anything. Just give me ten minutes, Superintendent."

She turned back to empty her glass, then went into the bedroom with her maid, closing the door behind her.

Left alone with the Superintendent, the pale-haired singer, Lélia, tried to find a topic of conversation.

"She's such a fine girl!" she said at last, sighing. "You'd never think, to look at her, that she risks her life every week and often several times a week."

Monsieur Charon's glance roamed over the walls, and he was surprised to see not a single photograph of Sophie Emel, who not only held five or six world records for parachute jumping but also piloted fast planes and raced at Montlhéry.

There were plenty of photographs, almost all signed, but they were those of pilots, sports personalities, stars of stage and screen.

The door opened a crack, and Sophie called out:

"Give him something to drink, Lélia. Now that it's practically apéritif time, perhaps's he'll accept."

"What'll you have?"

"I'll have the same," he said, pointing to the bottle of Scotch.

"I wonder what her grandmother will do. . . ."

Outside, the snow was still falling; occasional white flakes melted on contact with the ground or the rooftops. The Seine was the greenish-gray color of old bottles, and between its two branches the dark silhouette of a fisherman was outlined against the stone spur.

Sophie Emel reappeared quickly. She had put on shoes and a dark wool dress, under a raincoat lined with fur. The Superintendent wondered if it was mink. He had heard of mink-lined raincoats and had found this unbelievable, but nothing would have surprised him about this girl, who stood bareheaded and disheveled, her hands thrust into her pockets.

"Shall we go?"

"After you."

"Aren't you going to finish your drink?"

"No, thanks."

"You're lucky," she said lightly and carelessly, pouring herself some more Scotch, which she tossed off in one swallow.

Then, almost gaily:

"Let's go and see Grandmother!"

Because of the weather, the streets were relatively empty, and there was only Pont Marie to cross and Rue des Nonnains-d'Hyères to go down before they reached Rue de Jouy. Four or five people turned to look at the young woman, wondering whether she were indeed the person about whom the newspapers had so much to say.

Several buildings in the neighboring streets were shored up, and gaps between the houses showed where the demolition men had been.

On Rue de Jouy three men were waiting, making an occasional upward glance.

"There are more of them. At one point I thought of the fire department, but . . ."

She tossed her head to shake the drops of water

15

from her hair, and followed the Superintendent along a dark passage where old newspapers and trash of all kinds lay on the ground, as though the house had become the garbage dump of the neighborhood. On the first landing a policeman on duty handed his chief a flashlight. This was certainly needed, because the windows had been boarded up, a number of steps were missing, and the railing had been torn down.

Two men on the floor above touched their hats and watched them go past in silence.

The rooms had no doors; the gaps revealed faded wallpaper, which seemed to have been wantonly stained and soiled, broken mantelpieces, holes in the floor. Sophie commented as she tripped over an empty can:

"Well, here's one she didn't throw out the window."

The place was drafty, and the walls, formerly whitewashed, were scrawled with obscene graffiti.

"I'm sorry about this," the Superintendent apologized, quickly directing the beam of his flashlight elsewhere. "One more floor. Would you rather I let you go up alone?"

He had the impression that she was looking paler, but it might have been from climbing the stairs.

"I don't mind either way."

"Suppose I wait here."

Shrugging her shoulders, she went on, with her hands still thrust in her coat pockets, tossing her head again to throw back the hair that hung over her forehead.

On the fifth floor only one door was still in place.

Maybe the old woman had burned the other two, part of the frames of which were also gone.

The Superintendent, standing motionless in an uncomfortable position, since he did not want to lean against the wall, and there was no railing, listened intently, surprised by the silence, which was lasting longer than he had expected. At last he heard a match struck; presumably Sophie was lighting a cigarette. She gave a little cough, and said in a voice that was somewhat hesitant:

"Are you there, Grandmother?"

Nothing stirred.

"I know you're there. Do you recognize my voice?"

Still no sound from the other side of the door.

"It's Sophie talking to you—one of the twins, as you used to call my sister and me."

There was a slight noise. The old woman must have gone up to the door to hear better, since the buses were making the walls of the house rattle.

"First of all, how can I be sure it's really you?"

The voice was firm and surprisingly shrill.

"Of course! I forgot that my voice must have changed. Shall I remind you what happened in November 1944? . . . One evening Adrienne and I, coming home after school, announced that a man was prowling around near the house. We'd noticed him the day before, and the day before that. . . .

"I added that although he was slouching along like a tramp he wasn't too badly dressed. . . . Father went to look out the window, and declared that he couldn't see anyone. Yet he looked worried. . . . Do you remember? . . . He was afraid somebody was after him, because of certain books he had published during the war. . . . A few days after the Liberation, one of his colleagues, in the same situation, had been struck down on the sidewalk as he was leaving his office. . . .

"You had flu, but you were eating with us just the same. You were always hungry. . . ."

She fell silent. On the other side of the door the old woman was silent, too, and when she spoke at last it was to inquire suspiciously:

"What have you come here for?"

Then, her voice shrill and harsh: "To bring me a parachute, maybe?"

"I was told only this morning that you were still alive."

"By whom?"

"By the Superintendent."

"Is he with you?"

"Not on the landing. Down below."

"So that's what he was concocting! I wondered why they were leaving me alone. Tell him he's making a big mistake if he fancies I'm coming out."

"Why are you so determined to stay in there?"

"You're too young to understand, my girl. And perhaps, to judge by the little I know about you, you'll never understand. This is my home, my own little corner, the place I've lived in and come back to, the place where . . ."

The sentence remained unfinished, and there was a long silence.

"Are you still there?" the old woman asked at last, almost timidly.

"Yes."

18

"Did the Superintendent tell you that if they break down the door, I'm going to jump out the window?"

"He told me so."

"I shall do it."

"I know."

"How do you know?"

"Because I might perhaps do the same thing."

"You?"

"Why not?"

"Your mother, now, wouldn't be capable of it. Where is she, your mother? Is she still living?"

"She's built herself a villa on the Riviera, at Mougins."

"Does she live alone?"

"I don't know."

"You don't see her nowadays?"

"Seldom."

"And Adrienne?"

"My sister's married and has two children. Her husband is chief private secretary in the Ministry of Finance."

"Why didn't they go and fetch *her*?"

"I couldn't say. I suppose they haven't discovered that she's your granddaughter. Or else they didn't dare."

"Well, thank you for taking the trouble. Go and tell them it makes no difference."

"They're going to start knocking down the house tomorrow."

"Let them knock. I shall tumble down with the walls."

Hearing nothing more, the Superintendent wondered whether to go up a few steps. But the girl's silence was deliberate.

Her ruse succeeded, for a small voice rose again behind the door.

"Sophie!"

"Yes."

"I thought you'd gone."

"I'm still here."

"What are you waiting for?"

"What about you?"

"Oh, me—I have nothing more to wait for. That's what makes them so mad. They know that I don't care if I jump out of the window or have the roof crashing down on my head. So as a last resort they sent for you, counting on you to get me out of here and take me to a home."

"Why to a home?"

"Didn't they mention that? They even got a doctor to come and ask me questions through the door. They think I'm crazy. Perhaps you think so, too?"

"No."

"They'll shut me up just the same. There's nothing else they can do with me."

"Why can't you live somewhere else?"

"For one thing, I've got hardly any money left. More to the point, I don't want to live all alone."

"Aren't you alone here?"

"That's different. You couldn't understand."

An unexpected question suddenly proved that the old woman was peering at Sophie through the keyhole.

"Is that fur, underneath your raincoat?"

20

"Yes."

"Is it mink?"

"Yes."

"Well, you can go home now. Who do you live with?"

"Sometimes alone, sometimes with a girl friend."

"Never with a man?"

"Not so far."

"How old are you? ... Wait a minute. ... Let me figure ..."

"Twenty-seven."

"The chances are you won't get married."

"I'm sure I will never get married."

"Are you unhappy?"

"I never ask myself that question."

"You will, later on. Good-bye."

"Am I boring you?"

"It's you who must be fed up with standing on that drafty landing. *I*'ve got a chair to sit on. Have you had lunch?"

"Not yet."

"Nor have I. In honor of your visit, I'm going to treat myself to a can of crayfish."

"We could go to my place and eat something."

"I can see what you're after."

"I live a stone's throw away, on the Ile Saint-Louis."

"How long have you been there?"

"Three years."

"Funny we never met. Adrien and I often used to walk around the island with the dog. Poor beast. It died of old age six months after its master, and right up to the end I used to walk it along the embankment. . . . I may have gone past you without recognizing you. . . . And yet I've often seen your picture in the papers. . . . Your mother can't be pleased at your doing that job."

"Listen, Grandmother . . ."

"I won't go to a home."

"I'm not talking about a home. I could rent an apartment for you."

"No."

"What about my place?"

"*With* you?"

"Well, I've no intention of moving out to make room for you."

"But your friend?"

"You wouldn't bother her."

"But I would bother you. You're talking like this now because we've just met one another and you don't like the idea of my jumping out the window."

"I'm twenty-seven years old."

"What about it?"

"I left home at eighteen."

"What did your mother say?"

"Never mind that. I've been living alone for longer than you have. . . . Perhaps we could get along together. Unless it upsets you to see me drinking . . ."

"You, too?"

A pause. Then, in a more human voice: "What do you drink?"

"Whisky."

"That's expensive. I make do with wine."

The Superintendent quietly went down one floor, and another. Listening attentively, he signaled to his men to move off. A few minutes later, he at last heard a door opening.

Still going down the stairs, he dismissed the detectives keeping watch on the sidewalk and, crossing the street, went into a bistro with steam-clouded windows and waited, standing at the counter.

TWO

Since, in fact, they were establishing contact for the first time and so much depended on it, every word, every gesture, every intonation counted, and the two women, aware of this, lived through these moments cautiously, as though in slow motion.

The Superintendent, in the overheated bistro across the street, where plasterers were eating their lunch, was puzzled on not seeing anyone leave the house. As soon as he had heard the key turn in the lock, he had assumed that everything was over— whereas really everything was just beginning.

Could he have suspected that the grandmother and her granddaughter, on the top floor of that decrepit house, had reverted to the instinctive prudence and the occasional immobility of wild woodland creatures?

Having turned the key and drawn the bolt, Juliette Viou had merely opened the door about a foot, doubtless deliberately. The gap was not wide enough to let anyone in. As far as she was concerned, the barrier was down. It was up to her visitor, if she wanted to enter, to push open the door.

In the same way, instead of scrutinizing Sophie, she had merely cast a brief glance at her, a glance that expressed no particular feeling, as though it were natural for the two women, after knowing nothing about one another for fifteen years, to meet again on this landing.

Sophie, for her part, made no attempt to go in, but stood waiting, as one might wait for somebody to put a hat on to go out.

"I'll soon be ready. . . ."

The girl could see nothing of the room but a section of white wall, which seemed, unlike the rest of the house, to have been freshly roughcast, the very clean red tiles on the floor, and, on a small cherrywood chest of drawers, a brass pot, a little framed photograph, a liter bottle of red wine, and a glass that still contained some drops of purplish liquid.

The old woman was hurrying to and fro, out of sight, alert and decisive in her movements. The apartment must have comprised two or three rooms, to judge by the sound of her footsteps, which grew fainter occasionally.

"Have you got your car down below?"

"No. I walked."

Juliette did not press the point, but it was obvious that she had not spoken at random, that there was an ulterior motive behind everything she said. She was

25

bustling about, lugging heavy objects, opening drawers and closets.

"Are you thirsty? I'm afraid I've only got red wine
to offer you."

"Not just now, thank you."

The old woman reappeared in Sophie's field of vision to fill herself a glass, which she took away into an
unseen corner of the room.

"You've got central heating, of course?"

"Yes."

"Even in the room that I shall be in?"

"Everywhere."

Sophie did not add that apart from her own room
she only had two tiny, badly lit bedrooms overlooking
the courtyard. They were listed on her lease as maids'
rooms, and Louise occupied one of them. The other
had hitherto served as a storage room.

"Hadn't you better fetch a taxi?"

"Why?"

"I shall have to bring some things with me. But
you're right. It's not worth taking a taxi. Pilou will
fetch them. If you wouldn't mind going to ask him to
come up for a moment . . . He's the son of the coal
merchant, the next house but one. . . . Are you still
there?"

"Yes."

"Are you getting impatient?"

"No."

"It won't take long. I'm being as quick as I can.
Those police fellows fancy that all the time they've
been watching the house I've been eating only
canned stuff. They're wrong. I've even got some
fresh bread left. Pilou used to fasten it to a string

26

that I let down in the evenings. And not only bread. Would you mind going down to fetch him? Tell him to bring his barrow to the door and come upstairs."

Sophie opened her mouth to speak, but thought better of it.

"If you go now, I'll be ready by the time you come back."

She went up to the chest to open a drawer; she was already dressed in a well-cut black frock and was wearing a hat.

The Superintendent, seeing the girl in the raincoat leave the house alone, thought that the experiment had failed and that she was going home discouraged. He was about to rush after her, but his hopes revived as he saw her going into the coal merchant's yellow-painted shop.

She did not stay there long. A boy of about fifteen came out with her and darted down an alley for a moment to fetch a barrow, blackened with coal dust.

The Superintendent, who had foreseen so many possibilities, had forgotten that of an actual removal. Nor had this occurred to Sophie, who now climbed back up the five flights without a flashlight.

The door was wide open upstairs, revealing the skylight, with its clean curtains, a round walnut table, and, all ready to be taken away, a huge black chest with a strap around it, bearing the initials A. V. in yellow letters.

"Ah, here you are, Pilou. Do you think you'll be able to carry this down by yourself?"

And, with an anxious smile, she explained to the girl:

"They're my things, you see."

Reassured by Sophie's lack of reaction, she went on to tell the boy:

"There'll be two large boxes as well . . ."

Her bright restless eyes kept darting cautious little glances at Sophie's face.

"After all, I'm not going to leave *them* the stuff I paid such a lot for. . . . You understand? I know you don't really need it, but it would give them too much satisfaction."

Pilou was dragging the black trunk toward the staircase.

"Is it fragile?"

"Not the trunk. Only the boxes."

She was now wearing a black cloth coat trimmed with marten, and she looked much less than her age, nearer seventy than eighty; she might have been any middle-class lady dressed for church on a Sunday morning.

"Are you quite sure you're not going to regret this, Sophie?"

Instead of replying, the girl asked:

"Shall we go down?"

"Just a second."

Time to go and finish her glass of wine, as Sophie had finished her whisky on Quai de Bourbon.

"I'll give Pilou his instructions once we're downstairs."

She was ready. She crossed the threshold. Did it occur to her that there was still time to change her mind? Standing on the frontier, she asked another question, which perhaps represented her final proviso:

28

"Would you mind very much if I brought my stove? A little cast-iron stove that doesn't take up much room, and keeps me company. Come in and see it, if you like. . . ."

"Pilou can bring it."

"You may think I'm a fool, but I wonder now if I could have borne to be parted from it."

She cast a furtive glance behind her, muttering to herself rather than to her granddaughter:

"I must tell him to take down the curtains and give them to his mother. I'd regret it all my life long if I left *them* anything whatsoever."

When they reached the sidewalk, the boy, with the help of a neighbor, hoisted the heavy trunk onto his barrow.

"Will you give me the exact address?"

Sophie gave it to her, and when Pilou came up to them, she realized that the old woman wanted to be left alone with him to give him her final instructions. So she moved away a few steps and pretended to study a grocer's window.

Both of them were still keeping their claws sheathed, and they had not yet looked one another in the face, as though that would occur only later, when they'd had time to get used to the situation.

Sure that she was being watched by unseen police-men, Juliette assumed a sprightly air, to show them that she had not lost the game, that she was not leaving under duress, but undefeated, of her own free will, with all her belongings, her granddaughter having come to get her and having invited her to live in her own home in a fine apartment on the Ile Saint-Louis.

Surreptitiously, she cast her eyes around in search of the men who had persecuted her, and when she came to join Sophie, she pointed to the clouded windows of the bistro across the street.

"I bet they're in there watching us."

Her next remark, apparently innocent, betrayed her immediate preoccupation.

"What kind of a car have you got?"

"I have three: a big American car and two Italian ones."

"Those long low ones?"

She was clearly wishing that a car of that sort had been sent to get her; that would have brought the neighbors out of their shops.

Rain was now falling, lazily and sporadically. The two women walked side by side on the narrow sidewalk and then turned right, leaving Rue de Jouy, where the demolition men could now get down to work.

For both of them, this was a difficult and dangerous moment. They suddenly felt the lack of the picturesque, dramatic atmosphere of the ruined house; and the vision of an old woman throwing herself out of a fifth-floor window was already fading. They were just two ordinary women walking along an ordinary street, on which they were constantly obliged to hug the wall or step off the sidewalk to avoid umbrellas.

Each of them had time to think things over and to feel disheartened.

"Do your windows look out over Notre-Dame and the Archbishop's palace?"

"Those of the studio and my bedroom do."

Sophie regretted having used a phrase which implied that her grandmother's windows overlooked the courtyard.

"For years I've seen nothing but roofs and chimneys."

The old woman added hastily:

"Oh, that suits me all right."

They crossed the bridge, leaning forward to face a sudden flurry of rain. In single file they skirted the houses along the embankment.

"Here we are. Come in."

The concierge watched them go past with much the same look that she had given the Superintendent that morning, the sort of look with which caged animals watch human beings parade past their bars.

"I'm on the fifth floor, as you were on Rue de Jouy, and there's no elevator."

When they had gone up two floors, the old woman commented:

"The house is decently kept."

She was barely out of breath, merely pausing for a moment on the fourth floor, not so much perhaps to get her breath back as from fear of the unknown place in which she was going to be confined.

She had avoided laying down too many conditions, mentioning the stove without referring to anything else, but she had given Pilou his instructions.

On the fifth floor, at last, Sophie pressed the bell. Louise opened the door immediately. Without saying a word to her about the newcomer, the girl ushered in her grandmother.

"Straight ahead."

31

Although the coffee cups had disappeared, the whisky was still in the same place. The open door gave a glimpse of the bedroom, which had now been straightened up, and the twin beds, with their buttercup-yellow silk spreads.

"Well, here we are! Take your things off. Louise, will you get the blue room ready for her?"

"What am I to do with . . . ?"

Louise had not yet realized the need to move with care, one step at a time.

"I'll see to that with you. Where is Lélia?"

"In the bathtub."

Lélia must just have finished her bath, for at that moment she emerged from the hallway, a naked white figure clutching a bathrobe. She stopped short, ready to beat a retreat.

"Oh! I'm sorry."

"It doesn't matter. Let me introduce my grandmother."

And to the old lady:

"This is Lélia. She's living here for the time being."

Lélia bowed in some embarrassment, and hastily made her escape.

Sophie explained.

"She's a very talented singer, although she works mainly in nightclubs. She's been rather unlucky. I'll tell you all about it. Sit down. Are you very hungry?"

It was ten minutes past one. Louise came in to ask:

"Shall I prepare lunch for three?"

"Yes . . . Wait a minute. . . . Have you got any canned crayfish?"

"Crayfish?"

32

"If you haven't any in the kitchen, go down and buy some, and make us a salad."

"Very good, mademoiselle."

The old lady, who was perching on the edge of an armchair, just as the Superintendent had that morning, tried to repress a smile of satisfaction, but protested for politeness's sake.

"You really needn't."

"I promised."

Sophie was standing in front of the bay window, and her grandmother was looking her up and down.

"I hadn't imagined you so tall."

"You forget that I was only twelve years old when you left us."

"That's true. Is your sister still as like you as ever?"

"Physically, yes."

Sophie went into the kitchen and opened cupboards with the preoccupied air of someone who doesn't know where things are kept. Successful at last, she returned carrying an opened bottle of Saint-Emilion.

"Will this do?"

"It's better than the cheap red wine I'm used to."

"Wouldn't you rather have whisky?"

"Not today . . . I'm afraid it might upset me."

Did this imply that it was too soon, and that she did not want to drop her own habits just yet?

"Tell me, before your friend comes back . . . Has she been living with you a long time?"

"About two months."

"And before that? Did you live alone?"

"Sometimes alone, sometimes not."

"Never with a man?" she asked, for the second time.

"Not in that sense. Not what you would call living together."

"Are you sure I'm not going to inconvenience you?"

"Since I'm not going to alter my way of living, you won't inconvenience me."

"May I take a closer look at your raincoat?"

It was still hanging over the back of the chair where Sophie had flung it. Juliette first felt the texture of the gabardine, then, respectfully, the fur.

"There was a time . . ." she began. Then, with a sudden switch:

"I suppose you've got another mink coat?"

"Two."

With a sly glance, as though to say "I thought as much," the old woman nodded approval.

"That's the sort of luxury I appreciate—the real thing."

She searched her handbag and took out two earrings studded with quite large diamonds.

"They belong to Prédicant's time. I had the complete set—necklace, clip, bracelet, even a watch to match. Don't you remember? On Boulevard Saint-Germain, when your mother was going out, she would come prowling into my room to borrow them from me, and she always counted on inheriting them someday. I sold the stones one by one when I needed the money."

She slipped the earrings into the girl's hands. Sophie, in order to show no emotion, went to the window to see them better.

"You can keep them."

"But . . ."

"I tell you they're for you!"

"Thank you. You mustn't feel yourself obliged. . . ."

"Nobody has ever obliged me to do anything."

Then, quickly changing the subject: "I bet your friend's dressed and doesn't dare come in."

She called out:

"Lélia!"

"Yes. What is it?"

"Aren't you coming back?"

Lélia appeared in the doorway, dressed in a close-fitting tailored dress.

"Why were you hiding?"

"I wasn't hiding."

"You ought to know that you're never unwelcome. My grandmother's going to live here, but that won't make any difference."

"You haven't forgotten that I have a rehearsal?"

"At three o'clock. That leaves you time to have lunch with us."

Sophie was pouring herself a drink when Louise, who had just returned from the grocer's, came in to announce:

"A young fellow has brought . . ."

Juliette sprang to her feet.

"It'll be Pilou! I'll go. Where is he?"

"At the back entrance."

"May I, Sophie? If your maid will just show me my room."

"It's got to be cleared out first."

In the end the three of them went through the kitchen in single file, the grandmother, the granddaughter, still holding her glass, and Louise sullenly bringing up the rear.

They reached a hallway that led to the back stairs, and in which there were three doors. Pilou was standing in the narrow passage with the big black trunk at his feet.

The old woman opened her mouth to speak, but Sophie forestalled her.

"Leave that trunk in the hallway."

"And the other things?" the boy asked.

Sophie did not bat an eyelid.

"The other things, too."

He hesitated:

"Well, you see . . ."

"What?"

"There won't be enough room. For the first load perhaps. But as for the second . . ."

"Show him the room, Louise. And then, if he has time, he'll lend you a hand to take up to the attic what there's not room for."

"Would you mind if I stayed with them?"

Sophie managed to mutter:

"Just as you like . . ."

And she hurried into the studio, where for a moment Lélia thought she was going to smash something or burst into tears.

Lélia had the tact to ask no questions, but simply went up to her friend, bottle in hand, and poured her a glass of whisky. Then, because the bottle was empty, she went and got another from the liquor cabinet and set about opening it.

"Thanks."

Twice, three times, five times Sophie walked up

and down the length of the studio, and, having regained her composure, stopped at last, with a mocking smile on her lips.

"That's that!"

"I guess I'd better leave you both to lunch together."

"Are you running away?"

"It's not for my own sake."

"I know. Maybe you're right. Shall I join you at five o'clock?"

"Do you think you'll be free?"

"I've warned her that I'm not going to change my way of life."

Louise appeared, stormy-eyed.

"Mademoiselle! She insists on having practically everything in the room taken up to the attic."

"Is the boy still here?"

"He's making a second trip, and I heard him say there might be a third. As for the old lady, she asked for a hammer and she's about to dismantle the iron bed."

Speaking to Lélia rather than to the maid, Sophie muttered between her teeth:

"She's brought her own bed!"

"What am I to do, mademoiselle?"

"Whatever she asks you."

When the door was closed, Sophie burst out laughing.

"There's an old lady for you! But don't ask me to explain."

Before flinging herself on the couch, she kicked off her shoes and sent them flying.

Of the three faces only one, the maid's, wore a dramatic expression. The old woman was as cool as she had been all morning, showing no trace of the effort she must have made to lug her belongings around and climb up to the attic three times, each time heavily laden.

When she finally returned to the studio, she was still wearing her black dress, enlivened by a white lace collar; in token of relaxation, however, she had changed into red felt slippers. She cast a rapid glance at Sophie.

"Isn't your friend lunching with us?"

"It's late. She has to be at her club at three."

A vague smile flitted over the old woman's face, the reflection of her private, heartwarming satisfaction at having achieved, in spite of everything, what she had decided to achieve. She took care not to speak about it right away.

"Will you go and join her?"

"At five o'clock."

Like a hotel waiter serving guests in a private suite, Louise now wheeled in a fully laid table, on which the rosy flesh of the crayfish could be seen.

The grandmother waited until the maid had left the room, then commented, lowering her voice:

"She's furious!"

"Why?"

"Because I upset her habits, and particularly because I've brought my own stuff. You don't object, do you? Pilou has promised to come back a little later to help me arrange my things and to fix the stove."

She ate hungrily, at the same time venturing to dart exploratory glances around.

"It's a very ordinary little stove, as you'll see. Or, rather, it was ordinary in the old days. Just a cast-iron cylinder on four feet. We bought it, Adrien and I, the first winter I spent in Paris, in 1902, from a second-hand dealer on Rue des Tournelles, and I can still picture Adrien, who was very thin in those days, carrying it home on his shoulders.

"At first the stove wouldn't draw, and the apartment was so full of smoke that we couldn't see one another. When we had put out the fire, we finally discovered that the chimney had been blocked by previous tenants. What a pair of fools we were!"

It was important not to alarm Sophie.

"Don't be afraid! Pilou knows his job, and he'll make sure that the chimney in my room is in good condition."

She was surprised at her granddaughter's calm, detached manner. Sophie acted as though nothing had happened since that morning. Perhaps the grandmother envied her capacity to keep silent, whereas she herself dared not let the conversation lapse.

"What your maid doesn't realize is that if I'm so anxious to get settled into my room and if I seem to be hustling her, it's just so that I can be out of your way and hers as soon as possible. Has the girl been with you a long time?"

"Five years. I had her with me even on Rue des Saints-Pères."

"Is she married?"

"She has been. Her husband left her. She put her two children in the care of a sister-in-law and went into service."

"Do you often eat at home?"

39

"Hardly ever in the evenings. I often have my lunch at three in the afternoon, and sometimes I don't have any lunch at all."

Two or three times during the meal their eyes met, furtively and evasively, each hastily glancing away out of discretion or shyness.

"Will you have coffee, Granny?"

"It seems odd to hear you call me Granny."

"It seems odd to me, too. Wasn't that what I called you on Boulevard Saint-Germain?"

"I think so.... Yes ... Anyhow your mother wouldn't have allowed ..."

She left her thought unexpressed. Her fixed stare showed that a sudden idea had struck her.

"Why shouldn't you call me Juliette?"

Sophie looked at her, at first with surprise, then with a smile of amusement.

"Call you Juliette?" she repeated.

Finally, tossing her head with a characteristic gesture to shake back the hair from her face and forehead:

"We can always try.... We'll see how we get on."

They had gone too fast, and it seemed better to talk of something else. Sophie was preoccupied with the question of the bathroom, which would have to be broached and which was a tricky one. There was only one bathroom, strictly speaking, in the apartment, and to reach it the old lady would have to go through the kitchen. In addition, the girl disliked the idea of sharing the privacy of her bathroom with her grandmother.

Down the hallway at the back of the apartment, beyond the maids' rooms, there was a rudimentary bathroom, which hitherto had been used only by Louise, and where the maid washed the delicate garments that were not sent to the laundry.

Might it not be best to say nothing and let the old woman do as she pleased?

"Aren't you jumping, these days?"

Sophie failed to grasp immediately that the reference was to her parachute jumping. When she realized this, she pointed to the sky, which was even blacker than in the morning.

"We don't do much of it at this time of year."

"And your car racing?"

"I may do the Monte Carlo rally in January."

"Will you look in on your mother?"

"I never go to see her. We sometimes meet by chance at Cannes or Juan-les-Pins."

"Has she ever been to this apartment?"

"No."

Sophie found it hard to believe that it was about the old woman's daughter they were talking.

"Has she changed?" Juliette went on.

"Last time I saw her she'd put on weight."

"She takes after her father. At fifty he weighed over two hundred pounds, and was proud of it."

Although dusk had not yet fallen, a fine haze hung about the studio. The newly cleaned towers of Notre-Dame stood out, chalky white, against an almost black sky. From time to time a tugboat's horn sounded, and pinpoints of light began to appear in the landscape.

"Haven't you got to dress?"

"No."

"But aren't you dining in town?"

"Where I'm going tonight there's no need to dress."

Juliette was listening attentively to every sound, and when she heard a bell ring in the kitchen, she sprang to her feet.

"That'll be Pilou. May I?"

"Of course."

"It'll take me some time. When you have to leave, don't worry about me."

Halfway to the door she turned around, somewhat awkwardly.

"I haven't said thank you yet. . . . I don't know if you'd rather I didn't, but I shall say it all the same."

"That's very nice of you."

"I'm not nice, and I'm too old to start now. Still . . ."

She deliberately kept her back turned and made her way to the door as she finished her sentence:

". . . basically, you see, I didn't really want to die."

Sophie, left alone, closed her eyes, and if she spent a little time in thought, she must have dozed off in the end, because when she sat up at last, darkness surrounded her, and the lights of Paris, seen through the window, were like a stage set.

It was ten minutes to five. She would be late reaching La Patate, the nightclub on Rue Washington where she had promised to meet her friend. It didn't matter. Lélia was used to waiting.

She did not switch on the nearest light, but groped for her shoes on the carpet and went into her bedroom to get the raincoat she had worn that morning, which was practically her uniform.

42

She had a bad taste in her mouth; she was familiar with it, and she also knew the remedy. Standing by the small table, she drank a mouthful of whisky from the bottle, while watching the streak of pale light under the kitchen door.

She heard voices, but felt no desire to know what was going on between her grandmother and Louise. She went quietly down the hallway and gently closed the landing door behind her.

The staircase, with its yellowish light and church-like silence, seemed to her more unreal or more alien than usual. She was apt, on passing the closed doors behind which other people lived, to stare at them with envy or hostility, according to her mood. From the first-floor apartment there filtered through, almost invariably, the soft sound of a distant music.

She hunted in her pocket for the key of the Italian car whose cherry-red bodywork was covered with heavy drops of rain, and a few minutes later she was breathing the smell of leather and gasoline as she switched on the engine and the windshield wiper.

Crossing Pont de la Tournelle, she reached the Left Bank, where she plunged into the stream of cars that, across the whole width of the quayside, were hurrying in the same direction, with faces as pale and blank as her own behind their windshields.

Then she drove around the Place de la Concorde and up the Champs-Elysées, where umbrellas jostled one another on the sidewalks.

On Rue Washington the nightclub sign was not yet lit, nor was the glass-fronted case beside the door, which contained photographs of the entertainers. The entrance was close by, and a little way down the hall Sophie knocked at a yellow-painted door, behind which someone was playing the piano.

A girl in black tights opened the door.

"Evening, Minouche."

"Lélia was afraid you weren't coming."

There were a couple of lighted lamps, great pools of darkness in the corners, four or five dark figures, the red glow of cigarettes, and the white shirt sleeves of the pianist, who went on playing while he waited for Minouche to resume her practicing.

Lélia came up to Sophie, looking tired, perhaps from too much rehearsing.

"How did it go?" she asked in a low voice.

"All right."

"No trouble?"

She seemed frailer and more timorous, more vulnerable, in these surroundings.

"Have you told them?" Sophie asked.

"No."

Minouche went on dancing, interrupting the music now and then to repeat a figure, with a stern, determined expression on her face. A stocky, swarthy Italian emerged from the cellar carrying bottles and put them down on the bar.

"So here you are! How are you, darling?"

He had shining teeth and a self-satisfied smile, and he called all the girls darling.

"Are you going to that movie cocktail party?"

"We'll probably look in there."

"Will we see you tonight?"

Sooner or later that night she would certainly come back and join Lélia. She never knew what she would be doing in an hour's time, and yet the same thing invariably happened. After that particular cocktail party, at which there would be three hundred people, they would follow a gang of friends somewhere or other, perhaps to another party, and eventually a small group would take them along to one of their usual restaurants.

At ten o'clock Lélia would rise from the table with a sigh.

"I've got to go to work."

Somebody might offer to drive her there; otherwise she would take the Métro.

Sophie would go along with some group or other to some place or other, and, probably, to yet another place, before ending up beside Lélia on one of the stools at La Patate.

And meanwhile on Quai de Bourbon her grandmother was resolutely organizing her life, and she had probably started bringing Louise to heel.

"Give me a Scotch!"

The old woman had asked her to call her Juliette. Why not?

It was really a joke!

THREE

In the apartment, which now seemed more than ever suspended in the void over the tip of the Ile Saint-Louis, Lélia, woman though she was, failed to understand the game that she saw being played by Sophie and her grandmother, a complicated game full of subtleties and nuances, of which they alone knew the rules.

They were living in a restricted world: next to the studio there was the bedroom, with its twin beds, the bathroom opening onto a hall, and beyond the kitchen a mysterious room, Juliette Viou's bedroom, which appeared to be the object of complex maneuvers—too complex, anyway, for Lélia, who, to her surprise, saw day after day go by without her friend attempting to find out what the old woman had done to that back bedroom.

There were just the four of them, their overt or hidden movements witnessed only by the motionless towers of Notre-Dame, four women each watching the doings of the other three, sensitive to the least change of tone, the significance of a silence.

Louise herself was becoming an important figure and assuming a dramatic air. Her original hostility toward the intruder was now less marked, though it was impossible to know what she was thinking.

It was on a Tuesday, in the middle of the day, that Juliette had been transplanted from Rue de Jouy to the Quai de Bourbon. The following night, actually about three in the morning, when Sophie and Lélia came in, nothing about the apartment betrayed her presence. Everything was in its place, and a single light was burning in the studio as usual. There was no unfamiliar smell and no sound.

They had looked at one another with surprise and satisfaction. Everything was going all right. The old woman must be asleep in her room beyond the kitchen.

And yet, once in bed, in spite of the distance that separated them from the back regions, Lélia felt compelled to whisper instead of speaking in normal tones.

"I think I'd better go and live in a hotel."

"No!" was all Sophie replied.

"It can't possibly work, the three of us. I'm not one of the family."

That was not the right word, but she could not think of any other. She was aware, in a confused way, that a game from which she was excluded was being played between the two women, as though they belonged to a race apart or had some old score to settle.

47

"Go to sleep. You're tired."

At noon Sophie got up first, without waking Lélia. She slipped on her tight trousers and her old sweater and, passing through the studio, she went into the kitchen as usual. Louise, who was sitting there alone, gave a start.

"I'll make your coffee right away. Is Mademoiselle Lélia up?"

"She's still asleep."

Sophie seemed to sniff the air around her, as though to catch some trace of an alien presence.

"Is my grandmother still in bed?"

"She's been up since half past six."

"Did you take her breakfast?"

"She didn't want me to."

"Hasn't she eaten anything?"

"She came in to get some bread and butter. Otherwise she's got everything she needs."

Sophie repeated, without immediately understanding:

"Everything she needs?"

"Yes. Ground coffee, honey, jam; she's still got some packages of rusks, but she fancied some fresh bread."

Louise was stating facts, without acrimony.

"You mean she's brought her own provisions?"

"I don't know how much she's brought. There are two large boxes full, one of them with bottles in it."

"Last night, did you serve her dinner in the studio?"

"She asked if she might eat with me in the kitchen."

Louise was already on the defensive, as though expecting a reprimand. When nothing happened, she went on almost defiantly:

"This morning she's begun a grand cleanup."

Lélia was standing in the doorway, in her pajamas, and noticing the old woman's absence, asked in a sleepy voice:

"Is she unwell?"

"She's having a grand cleanup."

"Have you been to see her?"

"What for?"

Lélia did not press the point. About half past one, when Louise wheeled the lunch table into the studio laid only for two, a questioning glance from Sophie was enough; the maid understood and announced, without giving any details:

"Madame Juliette has eaten."

She did not say "Madame Viou," or "your grandmother." There was a difference.

The old woman did not appear until after five o'clock, when Sophie was alone, reading on her couch. She came into the room so quietly that the girl did not notice, and was surprised to hear a voice quite close to her.

"Am I disturbing you?"

"Why should you disturb me?"

Juliette was wearing a flowered housedress, clean and bright and freshly ironed, and she had on her red slippers.

"Aren't you going out?"

"Not before half past seven."

She sat there, implying by her attitude that she intended only a brief stay.

49

"I've almost finished putting things in order," she said with a sigh of satisfaction.

Sophie was watching her over the top of her book, and while one of them issued no invitation to come and see her room, the other displayed no curiosity, no desire to go there.

"Don't you ever have visitors in the afternoon?"

"Friends sometimes come to see me."

"Without being expected?"

"Some are expected, others aren't."

"I heard you both come back at three o'clock."

"Did we wake you?"

"I wasn't asleep. I sleep very little, only two or three hours a night."

Were they aware that they would eventually broach more personal subjects, and were they deliberately, by tacit agreement, beating about the bush in the meantime?

"Your friend isn't very cheerful."

"She has no reason to be."

"That's what I thought. She seems to me to be one of those women who attract misfortune."

Sophie cast a sharper glance at her grandmother, who added, with no trace of sentimentality, as though stating an obvious fact:

"She won't make old bones."

"How can you tell?"

"I can feel it."

"What about me?"

"Unless you go out of your way, you'll live as long as me."

A silence that was almost palpable followed. When

Sophie was alone in the studio, in the late afternoon, she would switch on only the big standard lamp by her couch, which had a pink silk shade, and rosy shadows filled the room, where, in order not to shut out the flickering lights of the city, the curtains were seldom drawn.

Sophie went on talking for the sake of talking, in an unemphatic voice, as though speaking by rote:

"The doctors are pressing her to have one kidney removed. She keeps postponing the operation, because she's afraid she might not wake up from the anesthetic."

"She's been very poor?"

She seemed to be stating a fact rather than asking a question.

"As poor as in stories of bygone days. She was born in a village on the outskirts of Lille—I've forgotten its name—close to the slag heaps of a coal mine. Her mother was French and her father a Polish workman, who died not long ago in a mining accident. There were eight or nine children, and they often went hungry. The father was violent when he was drunk, and Lélia, possibly because she was the most delicate, was the one on whom he vented his anger.

"Her real name isn't Lélia, but Stéphanie. When she was fifteen she became pregnant, and her mother took her to a neighbor to get rid of the child. Subsequently, they had to remove, to use her own terms, all her woman's insides."

Thus Lélia unwittingly played a part in the two women's maneuvers and perhaps in their subtle mutual exploration.

"Did she run away from home?"

"Not even that. She's not the running-away kind. She stayed at home and, at seventeen, married a neighbor, thinking she'd get some peace. A man named Seveux—I know because it's still the name that appears on her identity card. He was ten years older than she was and looked gentle and timid. He was a model employee, and a few months later his company in Lille sent him to the head office in Paris."

All this was unimportant in itself, because they were not so much concerned with Lélia as with establishing contact.

"Apparently while they were living in Lille, Seveux behaved like a perfectly ordinary husband, what's known as a good husband. On Sundays he would take his wife to his parents' home, where sisters and brothers-in-law gathered, and once a week they'd go to the movies together.

"In Paris the only place they found to live was a sort of barracks full of screaming children at the Porte d'Italie.

"At the office, Seveux was promoted and was considered by his bosses to be the calmest and most reliable of their staff. But his character, at home, began to change.

"Lélia maintains that it all began with a slap in the face. One evening, for some quite unimportant reason, when they were going to bed, he slapped her face, and she began to cry. When he ordered her to shut up and raised his hand against her again, she was seized with panic and fled down the staircase half naked.

"He ran after her. Some neighbors joined in, and that was the start of it all, as though that evening Seveux discovered his wife's weakness, her capacity for suffering."

The grandmother listened without a movement, without a comment, her small eyes in a fixed stare.

"I suppose," Sophie went on, "that he also discovered the pleasure of tormenting her. On the pretext that she went after men, he used to shut her up before going to work. Then it occurred to him to lock up her dresses and shoes, which didn't prevent her from escaping when she wanted to.

"Needless to say, he let her have no money, and she determined to earn some. He didn't want her to work. I don't know what job she could have done, since she could barely read and write. She might perhaps have become a salesgirl. But for that she'd have had to leave home at fixed times, and he'd have noticed.

"The rest of the story could have happened to nobody but Lélia. She had noticed that at nightfall certain girls solicited in the streets by the Madeleine, outside the Trois-Quartiers store, walking two hundred yards or so along Rue Duphot, pretending to look at the shop windows, and then slowly walking back toward the boulevards.

"She tried it out once, without success. Nobody spoke a word to her.

"The second time, a man who passed her, walking very fast, suddenly stopped a few paces ahead of her and turned to look at her, frowning as though puzzled. She told me that if he had not been so well dressed she'd have thought he was a policeman and would have taken to her heels. He asked her straight out:

" 'How long have you been working around here?'
She was so taken aback that she scarcely lied.

" 'It's the first time.'
"Pointing to the door of a hotel, he asked her:

" 'Have you been there?'

" 'Not yet.'

" 'Come with me.'
"He took her not into that hotel but to his car, which was parked a little farther on and toward which he had been hurrying when he noticed her. As they drove through the crowded streets, he went on asking brief, specific questions.

" 'How old are you?'

" 'Nineteen.'

" 'Do you live with your parents?'

" 'I'm married.'

" 'Does he know?'

" 'No.'

" 'Any children?'

" 'No.'
"A little later, she was sitting opposite him at a table in a bar on the Champs-Elysées where he was well known, and where at this time of day there were only two or three couples, holding hands and whispering in the dimly lit room.

"You said she attracts misfortune. Well, that evening, Lélia lived through a fairy tale."

"Do you believe in fairy tales?" the old woman asked without a smile, as though this were an important matter.

Sophie did not answer her question.

"I knew the young man; we used to go to the same places, and he sometimes joined our gang. He had scarcely known his mother. His father had just died, leaving him joint owner with his sister of one of the most famous perfume factories in France.

"Alain, who was thirty-two and unmarried, fell madly in love with Lélia. At that time she was still Stéphanie, and it was Alain who, later on, chose a new name for her.

"She never went back to the Porte d'Italie. Alain set her up, to begin with, in a hotel near the Etoile and then, a few weeks later—she was already a different woman—in his apartment on Boulevard Richard-Wallace, at the edge of the Bois de Boulogne.

"The first time I met her she was with him in a nightclub, where, after several months together, they were still holding hands.

"I believe at one point she tried to become a fashion model. For one reason or another it didn't work out. She's always been obsessed by the desire to do something on her own.

"Once, they were in a small nightclub together, and, about four in the morning, when there were only a few regular customers left, Alain persuaded her to sing. That was how her career began."

"Did her husband never trace her?"

"Only much later, when he saw her pictures as Lélia in the papers."

"How did he react?"

"He wrote her heartrending letters, asking her to forgive him, imploring her to come back, taking all the blame on himself. Even now he sometimes waits to see her at the door of the club. He doesn't try to speak to her; he just looks at her with a woebegone air. She's afraid he might have a gun and might shoot her someday."

"And Alain?"

"He was killed just over two months ago, with all the other passengers of that plane from Stockholm that crashed in Denmark. The very next day his sister and her husband, accompanied by a summons server, burst into the apartment on Boulevard Richard-Wallace, and Lélia had to get out of the place with what she had on, leaving behind her jewels and furs and all the presents her lover had given her."

The old woman simply said:

"I understand."

She did not ask how or why Sophie had taken the girl in.

"And the husband?" she murmured presently.

"He still turns up from time to time on Rue Washington, where the doorman keeps an eye on him."

"Doesn't he ever come prowling around here?"

Suddenly Sophie, who had been talking at such length about Lélia in order to avoid dangerous topics, realized that she had touched a sensitive spot.

Had her grandmother noticed? Nothing in her attitude suggested that. Like certain women of an older generation, she sat upright in her armchair, without crossing her legs, showing no sign of fatigue, and giving the impression, even though wearing her housedress, that she was paying a formal call.

Was she, too, remembering another shadowy figure, the figure of a man who, long ago—only fifteen years ago—lurked in the darkness along the walls of Boulevard Saint-Germain?

Two twelve-year-old schoolgirls whom everyone, and particularly their grandmother, called "the twins," as though they had no Christian names, no individual personalities, had thought it a joke at first, and referred to him as "the tramp."

At first they had only talked about him to one another. He was their tramp, and they were loath to share their secret with grownups.

On their way back from school, as dusk fell, they would go by Saint-Germain-des-Prés, past Deux-Magots and the Café de Flore, from which, although wartime lighting was still in force, a certain warm glow emanated.

Immediately past that point, the sidewalk became more deserted, more mysterious, and the little girls guessed which would be the first to spot the tramp.

Sometimes he stood on the threshold of the house next door, so motionless that one could not see him until one was almost touching him, and that was frightening. At other times he limped along, hugging the walls.

He had a thick gray beard and heavy eyebrows, and wore a shapeless felt hat. He stared at the twins resentfully.

One evening, when he was not in his usual place, they discovered him on the opposite sidewalk, looking up as though in prayer at the windows of their apartment.

"Did you see?"

"Yes . . ."

"Do you think we ought to tell?"

"Maybe. You'll see, they won't believe us."

Their father was the person who showed most anxiety, and hurried to the window. Nobody thought of the grandmother, whose position in the household was practically that of an old-fashioned piece of furniture.

And yet three days later Juliette disappeared. Her daughter had gone out shopping that afternoon; her son-in-law must have been in his office, downstairs behind the bookshop. The two maids were questioned; only the younger of them had witnessed the grandmother's departure. She had even asked her:

"Are you going on a trip? Does madame know?"

The twins were at school. Sophie remembered her mother saying at the table, probably the following day:

"She's taken her jewels and all her belongings, but not her ration cards."

They had made use of these. They had even had them renewed when the time came, and Sophie, fifteen years after, was tempted to confess this to her grandmother to amuse her.

She dared not. It was too soon. Moreover, the old woman, who had been consulting her watch, now got up, saying:

"If you've got to be in town at half past seven, it's time for you to dress."

Sophie did not suggest that she should have her supper brought into the studio, realizing that, if Juliette preferred to eat in the kitchen with Louise when she was out, she had her reasons for it.

They came back late that night, she and Lélia. Sophie had been to the opening night of a show at the Théâtre Daunou, followed by supper at Maxim's. Her friend had joined her after her second show at La Patate, and they had ended up with a few friends at a nightclub as yet known to only a few initiates. They had all drunk a good deal, particularly Lélia, who was easily intoxicated, and who had taken it into her head to bring back a man whom they did not know but whose eyes, so she insisted, reminded her of Alain's.

She kept saying:

"I'm sure he'll understand me, Sophie. He looked at me just as Alain did that day on Rue Duphot. He's guessed. . . ."

"Come on!"

"Sophie! Don't be unkind to me. I know you're very fond of me, but, you see, there are some things that . . ."

She was almost weeping.

"Come on!"

Grasping her firmly by the arm, Sophie had almost dragged her out of the nightclub.

"Sophie, for pity's sake!" begged Lélia.

Then, in front of the open door of the red car, which the girl was refusing to get into, Sophie had slapped her friend's face, perhaps because of that recent reference to the slap her husband had given her, perhaps just because there was no other way of persuading her to go home.

This time Lélia became like a little girl again, whimpering in her corner.

"You hit me, Sophie! That's the first time you've

ever hit me! I'm not angry with you, and yet I ought to . . . I'm not angry with you because . . . because . . ."

And Sophie, with the particular perceptiveness of the slightly tipsy, cut in:

"Because you like it. Because you're made for it."

It was not exactly her grandmother's comment—that Lélia attracted misfortune—but it meant much the same thing.

"Sophie, tell me that . . ."

"Shut up!"

"Stop a minute, anyway, so that I can pee."

She had done so on the sidewalk in front of the Louvre, and nobody had seen her except the driver of a truck full of vegetables.

On Quai de Bourbon, Sophie had slammed the car door and then had to go back to switch off the side lights. Going upstairs, Lélia began talking again about the man whose eyes were like Alain's.

"Go on up!"

They made more noise than on the previous night, which was a frequent occurrence. Lélia undressed in the studio, scattering her clothes, while Sophie poured herself her ritual last glass of whisky.

"I'm not well. . . ."

"I know. We've done all we could about that."

"You'll look after me if I have an attack?"

Sometimes, and with increasing frequency, when she had drunk too much, Lélia would be seized with spasms in the chest, and her pulse rate would fall alarmingly for quite a while. At such times she was convinced she was dying, and earlier Sophie had believed it, too.

"You were quite right to slap me and bring me

home. I'm grateful to you. But will you please tell me what I'm doing here?"

"And what about me?"

Lélia stared at her friend, trying to understand and failing to. Then, since she was facing the kitchen door, she exclaimed, in what was meant to be a whisper:

"Here's the old lady!"

It was indeed Juliette, with her pewter-colored hair in curlers, wearing a fluffy red dressing gown that matched her slippers. She had undoubtedly heard Lélia's exclamation, but she gave no sign of having done so.

"I just came in to see if I could do anything to help."

She had taken it all in at a glance: Lélia, naked, with both hands pressed to her chest as though she was going to be sick; Sophie, in black pants and bra, sitting with her legs crossed in an armchair, sipping her whisky, apparently quite unmoved.

"Come into the bathroom," the old woman said softly to Lélia, as if it were the most natural thing in the world.

Sophie did not interfere. Leaning back in her armchair, with her knees raised higher than her head, she gazed distantly at the old woman, whose features were calm and relaxed, then at the young one, whose naked body, extraordinarily pale, was a wavering shape in the rosy lamplight.

Lélia had scarcely any bosom, and her hips and belly were those of an adolescent girl, as though she had stopped developing at the age of thirteen or fourteen.

After a spasmodic hiccup, she let herself be led away. Sophie sat there motionless, vaguely listening to the familiar sounds that reached her from the bathroom.

Soon afterward the old woman came trotting back. "Isn't there any medicine we can give her?"

"A sedative, to ward off the attack. The bottle's on her bedside table."

Next day when, about two in the afternoon, Lélia opened her eyes on hearing Sophie move about, she asked anxiously:

"Wasn't your grandmother with us last night?"

"She was."

"Was I naked?"

"Yes. It was she who took you to the bathroom."

"Didn't she say anything?"

"She made you take a pill, and then, when you were in bed, she said good night to me and went back to her room."

"Can *you* understand?"

"Understand what?"

Lélia, barely awake, was trying to follow her own thought.

"I don't know. Did she kiss you?"

"She's never kissed me in my life, except possibly when I was so young that I don't remember it."

"I'll feel ashamed in front of her."

"You don't need to. If it makes you feel any better, she's a red wine addict herself."

"How do you know?"

"She told me."

"I haven't noticed anything."

"Perhaps she doesn't dare overdo it yet, or else she hasn't felt the need of it so far."

"I don't feel well, Sophie."

"Go back to sleep."

"I feel rotten."

"Come in beside me. . . ."

Sophie had no need to repeat the words. With a supple leap, the pallid figure slipped from one bed into the other. Lélia huddled against the warmth of her friend's body and, with her head on Sophie's shoulder, she lay still.

At four o'clock Louise came in to announce that a man was waiting in the studio, an Italian manager with whom Sophie had an appointment which she had forgotten.

Lélia was so sound asleep that she did not wake, merely uttering a childish moan when her companion broke away from her. Sophie slipped on her narrow trousers and her old sweater, and lit a cigarette, which tasted unpleasant. She waited impatiently for the glass of whisky Louise had gone to get her instead of coffee, and when she had drunk a mouthful, she felt an almost immediate relief.

She was going through a bad spell. She had known others that had gone on for some time, but as soon as the flying season started, she was able to stop drinking almost completely.

The Italian had come to suggest dates and a list of the towns where he wanted her to work in the spring, and with him she was calm, attentive, self-possessed, laying down conditions, discussing figures and details of organization, down to the names of hotels and apartments to be reserved for her.

At one point she heard voices in the kitchen. No sooner had the visitor left than Juliette appeared in the doorway, looking as usual as though she were ready to withdraw.

"I'm not disturbing you?"

"No."

"Is your friend feeling better?"

"She's asleep."

"I hope she won't mind learning that it was I who looked after her." And for the first time she sounded a more personal note, with one brief remark: "I'm so used to it."

Perhaps if Sophie had helped her, she would have said more. But Sophie had no desire to hear more today, or, indeed, to talk about her own affairs.

"You've had a visitor?"

"Yes."

"Nothing annoying?"

"No."

"Do you have an agent, as stage people do, to look after your engagements?"

"I look after them myself."

"Aren't you going to eat?"

"Later, perhaps. Not right away."

"Would you rather I left you alone?"

"You don't bother me. If it amuses you, you can listen to records, or the radio."

"Haven't you got television?"

"I'm hardly ever here in the evenings. . . ."

But her grandmother was! Didn't that account for her question?

"Would you like television?"

"I've only seen it in store windows. I certainly don't want you to go to any expense for me."

There were books, too, five or six shelves full of volumes of every sort, higgledy-piggledy.

"Do you have to go out?"

"I never have to. This evening I don't feel like it. I don't want to have dinner here either, and Lélia, if I know her, will go on sleeping till it's time to go to her club."

"Won't you go to pick her up there?"

"Perhaps later. I've no desire to know what I'm going to be doing in two hours' time. If I don't go there, she'll just take a taxi. She has her own key."

An idea had just occurred to her, which was not particularly strange but which was in keeping with her mood of the moment.

"Do you know what I sometimes do when I'm by myself and don't want to meet people I know? I go down to the embankment, near Pont Marie. There's a little restaurant there for regular customers, with paper napkins and the menu written on a slate. Shall we go there together shortly?"

She was surprised at her grandmother's reaction: the old woman's eyes lit up and her lips quivered as she stammered:

"You . . . you're really inviting me?"

Her excitement was short-lived, soon interrupted by a little laugh.

"Don't, please, think yourself obliged to take me out. I'm so comfortable in my little nook. I can see you coming in and going out. I know you're there in your room. From time to time I go into the kitchen to ask Louise what you're doing. Last night we had a little chat together in my room. She told me about her lover, the butcher's assistant who comes to see her on Saturdays."

"Why on Saturdays?"

"Because that's the day his wife goes to visit her mother near Etampes. Every family has its own traditions."

Sophie had never suspected that on Saturday nights there was a man in the apartment. The old woman had been a fast worker! Of course she was not jealous of the intimacy between Juliette and the maid, just rather annoyed; and she was tempted to say nothing more about the proposed outing. However, she said at last:

"We'll go down about half past seven. The restaurant closes early, because the bar opens at six in the morning for the bargemen."

"What do you think I should wear?"

"Whatever you like. It doesn't matter."

"Will you put on a dress?"

"In summer I sometimes go there in pants."

Lélia slept the whole time Sophie was taking her bath and dressing. It was not until her friend was about to go out that she stirred and, with her eyes still closed against the light, asked in a faraway voice:

"Where are you going?"

"Out to dinner."

"With whom?"

"With Juliette."

"Juliette?"

"My grandmother."

"Where?"

"To François's. Do you want to join us there?"

"I haven't the energy."

"Go to sleep then."

"Tell Louise . . ."

"I know. To wake you at half past nine."

"Aren't you going to come and get me?"

It was a strange experience for Sophie to leave the apartment and emerge onto the embankment with her grandmother beside her, and then walk slowly, like an old-established resident, along the wet sidewalk.

The rain had stopped, and the air was sharp, with a few stars sparkling. In one of the neighboring houses a party was going on, and cars were queuing up as though outside a theater, women in cocktail-party dresses were setting out, their perfume drifting on the evening air, and the men were wearing dinner jackets.

The old woman's face was as excited as if she, too, were being taken to a party.

"Do you leave your car outside the house?"

"Only one of them, that red one."

"And the others?"

"One's in a garage on Rue Saint-Louis-en-l'Ile, and I leave the fastest one at Montlhéry."

Fifty yards farther on the old woman was still turning around to watch the people getting out of their cars and to look at the lighted chandeliers behind the tall windows.

"I remember a time when this wasn't yet a smart district," she said. "Now they say it's one of the most expensive in Paris, full of English and Americans. Did you find your apartment without difficulty?"

"By chance. Some friends who were leaving for South America."

"Did you get it furnished?"

"Partly."

"Is this where we're going?"

They had come to a restaurant, in the front part of which was a bar counter at which some workmen were drinking apéritifs. The proprietor, with his shirt sleeves rolled up, gave Sophie a familiar greeting and cast a curious glance at the old woman.

"Boiled beef today, Mademoiselle Emel."

And the grandmother whispered:

"Are you fond of boiled beef, too?"

They sat down in a corner. Only four tables were occupied.

"What wine will you drink?" the waitress asked.

Juliette ventured, after a glance at her granddaughter:

"I'll have some red."

"And you, Mademoiselle Sophie? Some Beaujolais, too?"

It was warm in the restaurant; smoke was wreathing in the lamplight, and there was a heavy smell of cooking. The waitress brought some rillettes and pâté, and, on a bed of vegetables, hot sausage, of which she cut each of them a thick slice.

Juliette, her eyes sparkling, could not resist drinking her first glass almost with one gulp.

"You know, Sophie . . . *I should really have died.*"

She was so happy to be alive, to be here eating and drinking, not alone but with someone looking after

her, that by her third glass of Beaujolais she was almost in tears.

"One day I'll tell you. . . . I don't know when it'll
be. . . . It'll probably take some time. . . . You're sure
I'm not boring you, that you're not sorry you asked
me out to dinner? . . . Since yesterday I've been thinking a good deal about your friend. . . . No! Let's not
talk of that now. . . . Do you know the couple under
the mirror, on the right, who keep looking at you? . . .
I can't hear what they're saying but they seem to be
speaking English."

A huge dark-green bowl of gherkins was set in
front of them, and the grandmother's eyes gleamed
even more brightly with wonder and greed.

FOUR

For nearly an hour, in the friendly commonplace little restaurant, they had just been two women enjoying their meal, with no other bond between them than the fact of being seated at the same table, steeped in the same anonymous atmosphere as the other customers, who, on coming in, seemed immediately relaxed by the warmth and the good smells, while others, slipping on their overcoats, left to resume the course of their lives.

Here, during a brief intermission, there had been no thought of past or future, only food and generous wine and a physical well-being in which to take refuge and which made them talk trivialities.

Then, like the rest of the diners, like thousands of people in Paris at the same time, they put on their coats again and passed through the door into the blackness outside, followed by the proprietor's cheerful good night, and were met by the silence and chill of the embankment.

Pont Marie, opposite them, was deserted except for a single hurrying pedestrian, and on the far bank of the Seine, beyond the sleeping barges, the old houses of the Saint-Paul district were huddled together, mostly tall and narrow and crooked, with few lights shining.

"I was really close to ..." Juliette began, searching among the moonlit roofs for the one that had 'been her own.

Hesitantly, like a small girl afraid of asking too much:

"Shall we go and see?"

They went along Rue des Nonnains-d'Hyeres, where radio music sounded from behind windows. A little grocery, such as are found nowadays only in country districts, was still open, displaying its shabby jars and boxes. At the corner of Rue de Jouy the shutters of the coal merchant's yellow-painted shop were fastened with iron bars.

"Look!"

A fence was up, barring the sidewalk, and half the road as well; a few posters had recently been stuck on it. A lamp was smoking, and when they looked up, they could see a gap in the row of house fronts where a roof was missing and one or two floors, the outline of which was visible on the party wall. The arm of a crane stood out inky black against the sky.

Nothing was left of what had been the old woman's home except some rectangular patches on the wall of the neighboring house, one white and one pink with peeling wallpaper, the black frame of a fireplace hanging in the void, and beside it the pale square of what had been the kitchen, with its twisted lead pipes.

"It was true, you see! The Superintendent wasn't lying. It seems they hang a huge iron ball on the end of the crane and swing it against the walls until they collapse."

She was not inclined to linger, but turned back of her own accord, without pressure from Sophie. She was not sad; on the contrary, she seemed to be reassured by what she had seen.

Once they had crossed Pont Marie again, the old woman asked no questions. By tacit consent they both turned left, before going home, and walked around the island.

From some way off they could see the cars still packed close together halfway over the sidewalk in front of the house where the party was going on, and the sparkle of the two crystal chandeliers, diminished by distance; and they could imagine the excited faces, the chatter and laughter of the guests.

Everywhere else almost total stillness reigned, with lights here and there in empty, dead-looking rooms.

"At Moulins, when I was a little girl, such stillness frightened me."

Then, after a pause: "Do you know what suddenly made me think of that? It was hearing our footsteps. I think it was the sound of my own steps that used to frighten me, and I always imagined that someone was following me. I sometimes stood still to make sure the noise had stopped. Didn't you?"

"Yes, on Boulevard Saint-Germain, during the war, when the streetlights were painted dark blue and people walked around carrying flashlights. You couldn't see the cars coming because there was only a narrow slit on their headlights."

"In my day there weren't any cars to be seen. There wasn't any electricity either, only gas, and at night the shop windows weren't lit up. There would have been no point in that, since there was nobody on the streets. The only lights I remember in the whole town were those of the Brasserie Parisienne, where my father used to go to play cards.

"One evening my mother fainted while I was alone with her, and I ran panting through the streets. I can still remember the two bay windows, with their ecru curtains, behind which one imagined mysterious goings-on.

"I wonder if my mother ever set foot in that brasserie. It wouldn't have been proper. I had a confused vision of musicians on a platform, marble pillars, a huge room surrounded by mirrors that made it seem even larger, and I remember the click of billiard balls, faces seen through a haze of smoke, waiters standing staring at me, the smell of beer and alcohol and cigars.

"Finally and suddenly I came face to face with my father, and I hardly recognized him as he sat there with cards in his hand.

"I wonder now if it was on purpose, out of nervous excitement or to attract attention to myself, that I shouted: 'Papa! Come quickly! Mother's dying!' "

She fell silent, because a woman of indeterminate age was coming toward them slowly, with frequent pauses as her dog sniffed at the walls, wagging its tail. They caught a glimpse of her face, and a little farther on Juliette whispered:

"Did you hear? She's talking to herself."

That enclave of solitude and silence in the heart of

Paris seemed to excite her, and maybe because it brought back memories she, too, felt impelled to speak to the surrounding darkness.

"Perhaps I was disappointed that my mother didn't die that night. Not because I hated her or wished her any harm, but just so that things might change, so that I wouldn't have to go on living in the same house with the haberdasher's shop and its sickening smell.

"It had been my mother's dowry. When she got married, my grandparents, who were still quite young, retired to the country and left her their business, the best haberdashery in town, on Rue de Paris, next door to the famous gunsmith's shop where all the sportsmen of the neighborhood and the local gentry went to equip themselves.

"In those days the shops stayed open late. We had supper at half past six, and no sooner were we at the table than the bell would ring."

She was on edge. She was trying to say something that her words could not express. She was groping after a confused idea, losing the thread of her thoughts.

"Look!"

As though it had some connection with her story, she pointed to a couple of lighted windows which revealed a high-ceilinged room, mahogany bookcases full of leather-bound books, and, above the back of an armchair facing into the room, the top of a yellowish bald head that did not move.

"Do you understand?"

"I think so."

"The feeling that everything's becoming fixed, that

74

the very air is turning into a solid substance that chokes one . . ."

They had come to Quai de Béthune, on the other side of the island, and here, too, in a private mansion, a party was going on, possibly a grand dinner, since two policemen stood by the door. The Seine was wider here. On the opposite bank cars and buses were following one another in serried ranks, almost as though it were daytime.

Juliette gave a short laugh.

"I wonder if that isn't why girls are in such a hurry to get married. At fifteen, didn't you long to get married yourself?"

"Maybe."

"To escape from our parents, from people whom we don't really know, from surroundings and a way of life that are theirs and not our own . . . I told myself that if my mother should die I'd live alone with my father, and I liked the idea not because he was my father but because he was a man . . . perhaps, too, because I would then take over his home. . . . Don't you think I've drunk too much Beaujolais?"

The previous night it was Sophie who had drunk too much, so that today she was feeling hazy and depressed. Two whiskies and a few glasses of red wine had been insufficient to revive her, and each of the old woman's remarks, pregnant with meaning, had infinite reverberations.

"Let's go up," she said, and sighed.

For one moment, on noticing her car, she had a crazy idea: to put Juliette in the car and drive off somewhere or other with her, to drink with other people, see unfamiliar faces, listen to random fragments of talk.

Well, it might happen someday. It would be rather funny. But they hadn't reached that point yet.

After a few steps under the dark archway, Juliette touched her arm to make her turn around, and she saw a couple leaning against the door, their faces pressed together mouth to mouth, while the woman's eyes met hers with indifference.

It made neither of them smile. The stairway light had been switched on, and strains of soft music came from under the door of the first-floor apartment.

"Do you know who lives there?"

"No."

Sophie had never seen that tenant, whoever he or she was; possibly a cripple or an invalid who never went out.

"Do you mind if I stop a minute? The wine makes my legs heavy."

On one of the landings Sophie happened to look into her grandmother's eyes and was suddenly struck by the impression that those eyes were ageless. This both fascinated and embarrassed her, as though she had just committed a theft.

Would it not be wiser for her to drink two or three whiskies and go out as she usually did? She hunted in her pocket for the key, since Louise had probably gone to bed. She promised herself to stay just long enough to get rid of Juliette and then to go out very quietly.

She pushed open the door and turned on the light. There was the studio, with its rose-colored lamp aglow. The old woman, without taking off her hat or coat, said:

"Thank you for such a pleasant evening. Now I'll leave you, since I suspect you're going out."

"I think I'll stay in."

"Don't you want to join your friend?"

Sophie had thrown her fur-lined raincoat over a chair and was moving toward the bottle.

"If you're sure I'm not disturbing you, I'd like to stay with you for a little while. Just excuse me while I go and take off my shoes."

When she had disappeared, Sophie shrugged her shoulders, irritated and disheartened, almost hating the old woman. Juliette soon came back, and her expression showed that she had hastily tossed off a glass.

"I didn't shock you just now, did I, when I talked about my mother and about parents in general?"

"Nothing shocks me."

"Have you never wished your mother was dead?"

"Often. Sit down. Some whisky?"

"Do you think I ought to? . . . A very little, then."

She was seated farther back in her armchair than usual. For a few minutes each of them followed her own train of thought, and the old woman was the first to indicate what hers had been. Characteristically devious, she avoided going directly to the point.

"Lélia, now, doesn't realize . . ."

She added, as though it had some connection with that tentative remark:

"By and by the girl we saw under the archway will go home to her parents and she'll probably hurry into her room to wash her hands for fear they might smell of a man."

Sophie, curled up on the couch, a cigarette in her hand and a glass within reach, was watching her companion's face. It seemed remote and ageless, and she stared at it thoughtfully, until she could see nothing of it but the eyes, beneath which lips were moving.

"How old was your sister when she married?"

"Seventeen and eight months."

"Had she had any affairs before?"

"I don't know. The two previous years we didn't go out together, and we each had our own room."

"And had you known men at that age?"

"No."

"Nor had I. Not at eighteen. Only at nineteen. I wanted, at all costs, to have a job, and well-brought-up girls did not work in offices in those days."

"What did your father do? They never talked about him at home."

"They must have talked about him, but you weren't interested. He was head clerk at the Préfecture. He was a handsome man. At home he didn't talk much. I chiefly remember him going off in the morning and coming back at night, invariably calm and somewhat mysterious.

"I wonder, now, if my parents loved one another. At that period it seemed to me impossible—for one thing, because they seemed to me too old; for another, because my mother, even for sleeping, always wore a flannel undergarment that gave her a sour, sickly smell. I was disgusted by the thought of her sharing a bed with my father.

"I didn't want to help in the shop, where the customers were all women, chiefly old women who stayed a long time gossiping in whispers over the counter. Since I'd learned to play the piano, I became assistant in a store that sold musical instruments, Demarie's, a dark, solemn place, full of gleaming pianos.

"I would never have been allowed to work in any other business. Music was something noble. And old Monsieur Demarie was a venerable figure. . . .

"There was an annex at the back of the courtyard where they unpacked the pianos sent from Paris. This was the job of Demarie's son, Gaston, who was thirty-two and had a waxed mustache. He got into the habit of taking me along to the annex as soon as his father retired for his afternoon nap.

"He went about it awkwardly, and it took him a whole month. I put up no resistance, since I was curious, rather than disgusted. Each time I was puzzled by the expression on his face and could not understand why, afterward, he would rush off without saying a word and avoid me for the rest of the day.

"The cathedral was visible from the shop, and eventually I discovered that every time he had taken me into the annex Gaston had rushed off to confession. . . . Do you believe in God?"

"I don't know."

"What was *your* first experience?"

After a silence the old woman added apologetically:

"If it embarrasses you to talk about it . . ."

"It doesn't embarrass me. Only, if I tell it, it'll probably sound different from the way it really was. And it's liable to seem significant, whereas it had no significance at all. Basically, things would probably not have happened that way if we hadn't always been known as the twins, as though each of us was not a complete individual."

"I'd never thought of that. It was partly my fault. Do you hold it against me?"

"It was nobody's fault, and you didn't begin it. At school, too . . ."

She sipped her drink, calmly, her mind working slowly and laboriously.

"Adrienne met a young man at the home of some friends of hers. . . . I'd decided that we should each have our own friends. In fact, I had practically none. I thought I was different."

"Everyone thinks herself different. I do; so does the girl we saw downstairs, and so does the old woman who was talking to herself as she walked her dog. Even Lélia! I'm sure you still think yourself different."

"What about you?"

Juliette shrugged her shoulders.

"Do you suppose one learns wisdom with age?"

"He was named Jean, Jean Arnonville, and I used to tease Adrienne by declaring she'd fallen in love with his name. The whole family was high up in government service; his father was a state councillor, one uncle was a public prosecutor, another a senator. He himself had studied law and political science, and he had an important position in the Ministry of Finance.

"For six months they were our only subject of conversation and our only visitors at home, and Mother thought of nothing but wedding preparations. I had been relegated to the background overnight, and nobody paid attention to me.

80

"He had an apartment in a house that was family property, near the Trocadéro, and he and Adrienne were going to live there after their marriage.

"It was there I went to see him one Sunday morning. I don't know if I was acting out of vanity or defiance or some sort of despair. It doesn't matter, and anyhow I don't want to know. I wasn't hoping for anything in particular, either that he would fall in love with me or that he would break off his engagement to my sister. He must have been out late the night before, because he had only just had his bath at eleven o'clock in the morning. He smelled of eau de Cologne, and I could see a patch of talcum powder close to his ear. He was surprised and puzzled by my visit. Thinking I must have brought some message, he came up to me in his black silk dressing gown. . . ."

Juliette wore an amused smile.

"Did you gain your end?"

"It wasn't easy. When he discovered I was a virgin, he began by begging me to put on my clothes again. Later he asked anxiously:

" 'What's going to happen now?'

"I answered calmly: Nothing. You're going to marry Adrienne.'

" 'But you?'

" 'Don't worry about me.'

" 'And suppose it's you I'm in love with now?'

"Wasn't that really what I wanted: that the memory of me should come between the two of them, so that every time they made love I'd be there as an unseen third?

"Sooner than be present at the wedding, I persuaded my father to let me go and study in the United States. After that I never lived on Boulevard Saint-Germain again, and if I happened to see my parents, I felt like someone who has already escaped from the family. In 1956, when my father died of cancer, I was in Spain."

Juliette was not satisfied; something at the back of her mind was worrying her.

"Would you have married him?"

"I don't think so."

"Has marriage never tempted you?"

"No."

"You've never tried living with a man?"

A shadow darkened Sophie's face, and she answered only reluctantly, as though being forced to look into some secret region of her mind.

"Never for more than a night," she replied with repressed resentment.

And looking her grandmother in the eyes: "When I need it, I'd sooner pick up a stranger. Does that surprise you?"

Without replying, Juliette rose and held out her glass.

"Would you give me a little more? Just a drop before going to bed. I'm afraid of having caught a chill on the embankment."

Sophie pressed her.

"Did you never do such a thing?"

"Not like that . . . But after all, I wonder if it's so very different. . . ."

A little earlier, Sophie had intended to cheat, to announce that she was going to bed and, once alone, to go off and join her friend. Now Juliette forestalled her, patting her shoulder for the first time, in a faintly protective gesture such as Lélia might have made.

"You need to go out. As for me, I must get to bed. I've talked too much. I'm not sure, but I wonder if when I used to walk my old dog I didn't talk to myself, too. Finish your drink, get up, and I'll just stay a moment to see you off."

A little later, when Sophie picked up her raincoat, Juliette asked:

"Do you never wear your other coats?"

"Seldom."

"And your jewelry?"

"When I have to."

"Guess what I was going to warn you about, silly old thing that I am."

"What?"

"Don't drive too fast!"

It was half past two by the time Sophie reached La Patate, and the crowd had begun to thin out. She looked tired and sullen, and as she passed the coatroom she rebuffed the attendant who offered to take her coat.

Lélia was sitting on a stool by the bar, in her usual corner, where she could lean against the wall. She frowned as she watched Sophie come in.

"Where've you been?" she asked in a low voice.

Sophie merely shrugged her shoulders and picked up, at random, a glass of champagne.

"Can't you guess?"

"Who was it?"

"Doesn't matter. Come along."

They went past the place where, on the previous night, Lélia had squatted at the edge of the sidewalk, but their mood was different. Lélia was tired, too, and Sophie's silence, which she dared not break, made her feel uneasy.

They undressed without a word, then Sophie took a long bath.

"Good night."

"Good night. Did you get on all right with your grandmother?"

"Let's go to sleep."

The last light went out in the apartment, and for ten minutes their bodies lay tossing in quest of sleep.

Lélia was the first to get up, at ten o'clock, because she had a dancing class at eleven. During some dinner a producer whom she scarcely knew had told her:

"As for you, my dear, you'll end up in the movies."

And as she looked at him incredulously:

"Not in drama or comedy, but in musicals. For that you'll have to learn to dance."

She had once been asked to sing, and she had sung. Now, twice a week, she took dancing lessons, in a gloomy school on Rue de Clichy to which she went by Métro, only half awake, her ballet shoes and her tights under her arm. Although she ached for twenty-four hours afterward, she persevered meekly.

A telephone call woke Sophie soon after her friend had left: a painter wanted her to come to a house-warming party at his new studio that evening. She accepted out of sheer laziness, and Louise, hearing noises, came in to ask if she wanted anything.

"Some coffee and croissants."

"Will Mademoiselle Lélia be back for lunch?"

"Certainly not before half past one."

She went to drink her coffee on the studio couch, surprised to see a blue sky and sunshine streaming over the towers of Notre-Dame. The Paris landscape, which had for so long been black and white, was a medley of bright colors; the barges and the white and red triangles on the bows of tugboats seemed newly painted.

She counted no fewer than six fishermen on the towpath of the embankment, and from time to time, laying down their rods and watching their corks from a distance, they stamped and beat their arms to keep warm. She even saw a tiny fish glinting in the light as it wriggled on the end of a line.

She picked up her mail, and the inky-smelling newspapers. Louise was hanging around, as though reluctant to leave the room.

"Did you want to speak to me about something?"

"I wonder if I ought to. Madame Juliette asked me not to mention it."

"Is she ill?"

"A little unwell, she says. She insists it's nothing serious, that she often gets this sort of chill, which affects her shoulders and back, like my rheumatism."

"Is she in bed?"

"Yes, nice and comfy. I lent her my little radio and I took her some magazines."

It might be a trick, or perhaps the old woman was exaggerating some trifling ailment in order to achieve her end. Hadn't she, the night before, casually hinted in the course of conversation that she was afraid of having caught a chill?

"Are you going in to see her?"

There was no alternative, and Sophie, lighting a cigarette, crossed the steam-filled kitchen and knocked at the first door down the hall.

"Come in, Louise."

Even that "Louise" rang false, since the old woman was sharp enough to have recognized her step.

"It's you!" she exclaimed. "And I'd specially given instructions that you weren't to be bothered."

She was jubilant, nonetheless, with just a touch of anxiety, like someone who has prepared a surprise without being sure that it will be appreciated.

Sophie cruelly pretended to notice nothing of her surroundings, to be concerned only with her grandmother, without observing that the room was changed.

"Have you taken your temperature?"

"I'm not feverish, or so slightly that it's not worth worrying about. I've taken a couple of aspirin and a drink of hot wine with a lot of sugar and cinnamon. I'll be on my feet again by tomorrow."

She was not lying down, but sitting up in bed, with a blue shawl around her shoulders. At her bedside the radio went on playing softly.

It was warmer here than in the rest of the apartment, with a different sort of warmth, and the little cast-iron stove was purring in front of the mantelpiece.

"Are you annoyed?"

"Why?"

86

"I don't know. Perhaps I shouldn't have done it. After all, I'm in your home, am I not?"

Sophie was disconcerted, for just by opening a door in her own apartment, as the old woman had pointed out, she now found herself in a different world, where she was merely a stranger. Before, she had scarcely set foot in this room, and she would have found it hard to say exactly what it had contained.

At all events, nothing of that remained. The glossy cherrywood chest of drawers which she had glimpsed on Rue de Jouy stood under the window, and on it was a blue vase belonging to the house, with a bunch of daisies in it.

Was it Louise who had brought in the vase and bought the flowers?

The frame that, in the crumbling house, had held a photograph was no longer there. No photographs were visible anywhere. Only a few objects—a brass ashtray of an old-fashioned type, although the old woman never smoked, a round ivory box, an iridescent shell, some framed eighteenth-century engravings—were evidence that the woman living here had a past of her own and had not totally repudiated it.

The most unexpected piece of furniture was a low easy chair of well-worn polished wood, standing beside the stove; its dark leather had been covered with flowered cretonne. A small mahogany table stood beside it. On the stove, water was simmering in a copper kettle.

Everything was as neat, serene, and peaceful as in a convent. The rug at the foot of the bed, made of many-colored scraps of material, introduced an old-fashioned rustic note.

It was hard to believe that the heterogeneous objects that Pilou had brought on his coal-blackened barrow had blended to achieve a total effect of such dignity and harmony, and Sophie caught herself looking for those boxes of provisions, suspecting that they were hidden behind the cretonne curtain hanging from a rod in one corner of the room.

"It's all I've got left after so many years. You understand?"

Sophie understood, but felt irritated nonetheless, perhaps precisely because she understood only too well. It was not as simple as the old woman tried to make out, assuming a childish voice so as to touch her granddaughter's heart, but well aware that she could not deceive her.

From their first conversation through the door on Rue de Jouy, all her actions had been premeditated; even there, she had already firmly decided that if she went to live on Quai de Bourbon, she would reconstruct her nook, as she called it, her own setting, her way of life.

And Sophie, who had always recoiled at the thought of finding a man—even a husband—around the house in the morning, was now sheltering an old woman who was fiercely determined to preserve her individuality.

As for Louise, who had growled like a watchdog the first day, hadn't she begun to change sides? The old woman had not been out that morning. The flowers were fresh and had not come there by themselves, nor had the scuttle of coal. The maid had never thought of bringing Sophie flowers except when specially ordered to.

The easy chair by the stove, even though it had a flowered cover, was not a woman's chair. A man had sat there for years, the tramp with the thick gray beard, with a bottle of wine within reach.

"I think I ought to have got up. . . ."

She did not mean what she said. Behind her every word lay an intention, more or less remote, which had to be figured out.

Sophie was practically certain that there was nothing the matter with her grandmother. It was a way she had found to induce the girl, without a direct invitation, to come and see this room of hers and breathe the Viou atmosphere—or, rather, the Juliette atmosphere.

She had won. Sophie was sorry she had let herself be caught, the previous evening, when her grandmother had, as it were, baited the hook by revealing a few secrets.

Juliette had got her to talk. She wanted to have Sophie at her mercy, naked and defenseless, as Lélia had been when she took her into the bathroom. Lélia had served as guinea pig. It was always with Lélia that the old woman began, introducing apparently anodyne questions that actually went very deep.

Standing by the door, Sophie managed to maintain apparent calm, and, although there was no smile on it, her face expressed none of the feelings that troubled her.

"Would you like your lunch brought in?" she asked in a polite, noncommittal voice.

To which the grandmother calmly replied:

"No, thank you. I've already eaten."

FIVE

At seven o'clock Louise had brought in the old woman's supper on a tray, insisting on serving her in bed, and Juliette had not refused, realizing that this was the maid's indirect way of thanking her for their tête-à-tête in the kitchen.

Louise was not surprised at the grandmother's wish to eat the provisions she had brought with her. On the contrary, she saw it as a sign of the sort of sensitiveness she could well understand, sensitiveness of the poor, who don't want to owe anything to anybody.

That evening a can of cassoulet had been opened, and the maid brought out a bottle of wine from behind the curtain.

Juliette's questions were always either innocuous or indirect.

"I suppose the young ladies have gone out?"

"From what I heard, I gather they've gone to visit a

painter who's just bought a place in the country, somewhere near Versailles."

"Sit down, Louise."

Louise would not have sat down in the armchair, but she accepted a chair beside the bed, so that she seemed to be nursing an invalid.

"I hope I'm mistaken, but I'm really rather afraid Sophie isn't very happy," the old woman said tentatively.

"I've often told her she'd have less worry if she wasn't always picking up lame dogs, if you see what I mean.

"Where I used to live there was an old fellow who used to take in stray animals. In the end he had more than forty of them, dogs and cats and even a half-bald parrot. I needn't tell you the house was so revoltingly filthy that nobody would go in there.

"He spent all his pension money on buying stale bread, offal, and bones, and people said he used to share the animals' food. Finally he died. For two days nobody noticed. When at last they broke his door in, they found him on the bed, half eaten up."

As she ate, Juliette watched the maid with her small flickering eyes.

"I'm not comparing his case with mademoiselle's. Still, the apartment never stays empty for long. I've nothing against this Lélia, but she's a poor weak creature who weeps more than most, for no reason, and before her there was a sort of gypsy who went barefoot from morning till night. That's where mademoiselle picked up the habit. But this girl's feet were filthy, and she never took a bath during the three months she spent here. . . .

"She'd sit for hours without speaking a word, specially when visitors came, and we'd never had so many of them in the house; they came in gangs.

"Then she'd ransack the drawers to find scraps of colored stuff—she'd even tear up a dress—to make herself fancy costumes, and if she couldn't find anything she'd make do with paper.

"They'd play her damned music. The rest sat around in a ring clapping and shouting, and she would spin around like a savage, stamping fit to dislodge the lamp in the room below, and writhing so you'd think she was possessed by the devil.

"It always ended the same way: she'd roll on the floor stark naked, her mouth twisted, her eyes rolling, till she passed out, and I used to wonder if she was an epileptic."

"Did they have a quarrel?"

"I don't know how or when they parted company, because at the beginning of the summer they went off to Saint-Tropez together. Then mademoiselle went to England for some flying show, and when she came back she was alone.

"To begin with, she's always enthusiastic, and I'd get the sack if I ventured to say that one of these young women blocks up the toilet by throwing things down it or uses table napkins for dusters.

"Then one fine day there are quarrels and cries and shouts, and apologies and kisses, until mademoiselle gets fed up and slams the door."

"Have there been many of them?"

"In five years I've seen a round dozen of them. Some of them have stayed for months, others just for a few days. An American woman who spoke no French stayed the longest. She was a painter and she used to splash paint everywhere. She brought in models, always men, who posed for her naked, but contrary to what you might expect, nothing ever happened between them. When she woke up, whatever the time of day, I had to cook bacon and eggs for her, and they were never just as she liked.

"With another girl, mademoiselle nearly had some trouble, and I believe she was really frightened that time. This was a Breton girl of seventeen, who'd come straight from her village to go into service and who'd already begun streetwalking along Boulevard Sébastopol. She'd seen nothing and she knew nothing, and she'd look suspiciously at the simplest things I gave her to eat.

"She didn't dare go out of the house, because a police officer had threatened to pick her up if he met her on the sidewalks again. I used to go and buy short novels for her, and magazines with actresses' confessions, and I often saw her weeping over them.

"Then one morning we had a visit, not from the police, but from her mother, a stout pug-nosed woman, who started shouting and threatening. I was afraid she'd bring out all the neighbors. Finally mademoiselle gave her some money, and she took her daughter away.

"I'd opened the door a crack and I saw her stop on the landing below to count the money. ..."

"You'll take a drink of wine with me, won't you, Louise?"

"Not just now, but, since you're so kind, after I've

done the washing up. Provided you're not asleep, of course."

"You know I sleep so very little."

Louise, who slept in the next room and could hear her neighbor snoring, knew this was a lie, but did not hold it against her. She had been brought up to respect old people, particularly when, like Juliette Viou, they had had misfortunes and borne them with dignity.

Perhaps in her heart of hearts she was not really taken in by this apparent dignity, for she was a woman, too, and she saw what was going on. Nonetheless she took pleasure in indulging a grandmother whom a rich and rather crazy girl had relegated to a servant's room and who, instead of complaining, behaved so tactfully and with such consideration toward the maid herself.

Later on they sat together in the warm, quiet room, where, before long, the kettle of water began to sing; the lid quivered, a jet of steam spurted from the curved spout, and, at Juliette's request, the maid prepared two bowls of mulled wine.

They listened to the radio in silence, in a state of euphoria. At last Louise rose and picked up the empty bowls.

"It's time I went to bed. Wouldn't you like me to straighten your bed up a bit?"

Everything was dark when Juliette woke up with a start. Doors were banging, music sounding; the rhythmical beat of feet made the floor shake as though an entire wedding party were dancing.

She switched on her bedside lamp and saw on her alarm clock that it was twenty-five minutes past four.

People were talking loudly in the kitchen, men and women. The refrigerator was being opened and closed, the faucets were running, all this against a background of noisy music and stamping in the studio.

Silently the old woman got up, pulled on her dressing gown and slippers, and turned off the light before creeping into the hallway.

It had all started with the housewarming at the painter's studio at the beginning of the Chevreuse valley. At one point, about eight in the evening, there had been over a hundred and fifty people present, including a number of actors and actresses who had left early for their evening performance.

They had begun with whisky and champagne, with canapés, as at a fashionable reception, but by nine o'clock somebody had emerged from the kitchen brandishing a salami and a bottle of Chianti.

A few minutes later almost everyone was drinking Italian red wine, of which there was a copious amount in the house.

The guests, some in day clothes and others in evening dress, were eating sausage, with or without bread, some sitting on the floor, seven or eight of them installed on the painter's bed, where a woman was lying whom nobody knew and who, feeling sick, had removed her pants and brassière.

Sophie was drinking only whisky and relatively little of that; most of the time she stayed alone in a corner, gloomily observing all the excitement.

Lélia came up to ask her:

"Are you bored?"

"I'm watching."

"Are you thinking about your grandmother?"

Sophie glanced at her coldly but made no reply.

"Aren't you going to drive me to La Patate?"

"There's bound to be someone's car to take you."

In the general hubbub she did not see Lélia again and concluded that she must have found a ride. Several couples were dancing. Some glasses got broken. A smell of burning caused near-panic at one point, until some starlet suddenly tore down one of the curtains which had caught fire.

Most of the guests were well known in some field or other, and there were a few journalists and television people.

The numbers dwindled to thirty, then to twenty, no longer scattered through the huge house but all—except for two couples who chose solitude—collected in the studio.

It was the time of night when partygoers look at one another and wonder what to do next.

Somebody suggested the name of a new nightclub on the Left Bank, and a voice protested:

"It'll be crammed, and we won't all get in."

Other places were mentioned, and objections raised in each case.

"Why shouldn't we all descend on Marcelle?"

This was the mistress of a politician, who had lived for years in an apartment in Passy, where she could never bring herself to furnish more than a couple of rooms. There was bound to be liquor there, and Marcelle, even when you got her out of bed at three in the morning, was always game for fun. You could break everything and make a mess without her losing her temper, even if the party went on for two days and two nights, and there had apparently been one famous one that had lasted a whole week.

"Marcelle flew to London yesterday."

That meant that her friend had been sent there on official government business.

Then, perhaps remembering her grandmother and moved by a secret desire to infuriate her, Sophie had raised her hand.

"Why not my place?"

There was at least one case of whisky in the apartment, enough vodka and vermouth for cocktails, and probably some bottles of champagne.

"All those in favor?"

"Carried unanimously!"

"Have we enough cars for everybody?"

"Who doesn't know the address?"

"I don't."

"You've only got to follow us."

Three cars drew up first, one after the other, on Quai de Bourbon. The slamming of doors broke the silence of the night, and snatches of talk re-echoed as though in a cavern.

Another car braked noisily ten minutes later, and the occupants stopped at the fourth floor by mistake, waking up the English couple who lived there and embarking on a somewhat confused argument on the landing, which nearly degenerated into a fight.

On the fifth floor the party was under way. The record player was going at its loudest, at least four of the women had taken off their shoes and stockings to dance, and a tubby little man who wrote the gossip column in a daily paper had commandeered the kitchen with a friend and was mixing cocktails "à la dynamite."

Mink coats were strewn on the floor in the hallway, somebody was shut up in the bathroom, and the bedroom was serving as annex to the studio.

Sophie went on drinking just enough to keep herself going, with the same detached expression in her eyes she had had in the painter's studio.

"Hey, where's Lélia?"

"She's gone to La Patate to sing her piece; she'll be back soon."

"Shall we call her up?"

There was no time to answer one question before somebody else pounced on you. A banker's daughter, who wanted to get into the movies and had finally secured her parents' consent, was the wildest of all. She was barely eighteen, with an ambiguous plumpness that was no longer the puppy fat of adolescence and not yet the curves of a mature woman.

"They say Lélia left in a taxi a quarter of an hour ago."

Nobody saw her come in. She must have used her key.

In the back hall, Juliette was listening, her ear against the wall, occasionally bending down to peer through the keyhole, and meanwhile watching Louise's door, under which she expected to see a light.

Twice, she stepped back a few paces because Sophie came into the kitchen as though she intended to go farther, and the old woman felt practically certain that the girl knew she was there.

"A dance, Lélia!"

They had seen Lélia at last. The whole thing was following a familiar routine, in which everyone always played more or less the same role.

"In tights! In tights!"

Lélia meekly went to put on the black tights she wore at her dancing class. She was under no illusion. By the time she was dressed up, they would probably have forgotten all about her dance.

"Hey, Sophie . . ."

"What is it?"

"We're all getting a bit hungry."

They had had nothing since the painter's canapés and salami.

"Let's make a fabulous spaghetti!"

"Let me!"

Five people rushed into the kitchen, rummaged in drawers and cupboards, but found only half a package of spaghetti.

At that point Sophie called for silence and announced, with a slight quiver of her lips:

"What would you say to a surprise supper party?"

Some people shouted yes enthusiastically, others waited to hear more.

"Somewhere in the apartment there's a box full of canned stuff. I don't know exactly what. I'll bring it in and everyone can take his pick. How's that?"

"No! Let everybody pick at random with their eyes shut."

Just as on Rue de Jouy, there was a closed door between the two women, but this time the roles were reversed. The old woman was now outside, listening, anxious and pale-faced, while Sophie was in command and laid down her conditions.

She met Lélia's uneasy glance and thought she read in it disapproval, even entreaty, but now that she had started it was too late to draw back.

"Where's the box?"

"I'll go and get it."

"Sophie!" ventured Lélia.

"Shut up, you!"

The journalist followed her. "Let me help you carry it."

"No. I'm going alone."

She had spoken loudly on purpose. And so the old woman had been warned. In fact, Juliette showed herself a good loser. Instead of going back to bed and pretending to sleep, she waited in front of her door for her granddaughter.

"Behind the curtain," she said a little hoarsely.

And she added:

"I doubt whether you'll be able to carry it by yourself. It's very heavy."

"I can always drag it."

She was stronger than her grandmother had thought, because she managed to lift the box.

"Don't you want the bottles, too? There are some in the other box."

"No, thanks."

The joke lasted for a few minutes only. Each in turn, with closed eyes, the guests dipped into the box, and drew out cans of sardines, tuna fish, asparagus, peas, or mackerel in white wine. There was more mackerel than anything else, eight or ten cans of it, a cheap brand sold on special offer in local groceries.

They hunted for a can opener. Some people gave up. Those who had been eating with their fingers wiped them on the curtains; one sardine lay for a long time in the middle of the carpet. Lélia finally picked it up and threw it into the garbage can.

When eventually someone remembered that Lélia had been asked to dance, and when they had all gathered around in a ring, the banker's plump daughter, who was drunker than anyone else, stole the show by dancing beside her with her skirt lifted up to the waist.

Sophie had now started drinking in her corner, determined to throw the whole crowd out if things went on too long. She was the only person who took note of what was happening, and she knew which two couples, each in turn, withdrew into her bedroom.

She saw Lélia open the door to go in and change, then stop short and step back, because the people there went on making love, not even noticing her.

Some guests left without bothering to say goodbye. The toilet flushed repeatedly. In the kitchen the gossip columnist persisted in mixing cocktails, which nobody drank and which stood about unwanted on the furniture.

Through the bay window, lights could be seen in a few houses, less bright than the light that outlined the walls; gradually there were more and more of them. Bistros were opening, shadowy figures moving on the decks of moored barges. Buses and cars, at first sparse, came to form an almost continuous line along the other bank.

Soon there were only five people left, then only three.

"What are we to do with Francine?"

The bedroom door was wide open, and the young girl lay there asleep, on Sophie's bed, her thighs bare, one rosy breast outside her slip. Her partner had disappeared, and so had the other couple who had taken advantage of the bedroom.

"Francine!"

"What is it?"

"Time to go."

"Where are we going?"

"We're taking you home."

She sat up, puzzled at finding herself on a bed with three people looking at her.

"All right, I'm coming. Just give me back my dress."

Lélia helped her to dress and brought her a damp towel.

Sophie escorted the last remaining group to the door, which she locked behind them. When she returned to the studio, she found Louise, who had just got up to start her work, in tight-lipped silence.

She shrugged her shoulders and went into her bedroom, carrying a bottle. Lélia could at last take off her sweat-soaked tights. Locking the door in the servant's face, vindictively, Sophie began undressing, too.

"Do you want a drop?"

"No, thanks. I'm too tired."

Sophie drank, however, with her gaze fixed on her friend, then she said:

"I don't want to hear a word from you."

"I've got nothing to say."

With anyone other than Lélia a scene would have taken place, and Sophie would probably have got rid of a humiliating witness. Lélia, however, offered one no handle. A member of the gang, one day when he was not tipsy, had christened her the Immaterial One.

A thin slit between the curtains was turning dull white, then silvery. For most people, day was beginning.

"Of course it was *my* bed they chose, the pigs!"

"Would you like mine?"

"Lie down and leave me alone."

It was only at nine o'clock that Louise, methodically performing a task with which she was not unfamiliar, and from time to time going to listen at the old woman's door, thought she heard a peculiar murmuring sound.

She opened the door cautiously and found the grandmother sitting up in bed weeping.

There was no sign of life in the girls' bedroom until five o'clock, when Lélia came out on tiptoe and went to the bathroom with her shoes in her hand and her clothes over her arm. She had an audition at six o'clock at a music hall.

She had been hoping for a long time for an engagement there and she was alarmed at the thought of appearing in such poor shape.

While she was in the bathtub Louise knocked on the door and went in.

"Can I get you something to eat, Mademoiselle Lélia? You mustn't go out on an empty stomach."

"I'm not hungry."

"I'll beat you up a couple of eggs in sweetened milk."

"Milk makes me feel sick."

"I'll beat them up in port wine, if they've left any."

The apartment had resumed its usual appearance, with a few damp marks on the carpet and on the armchairs and curtains, where the maid had tried to remove stains.

"What's the weather like?"

"Its fine, but very cold. The sun's been shining all day."

"Is my voice very hoarse?"

"It'll be all right in half an hour."

"You know, Louise, none of it was my fault."

"I know."

"How is she?"

There was no need to mention Juliette's name.

"I did my best to cheer her up. She's remained so active and so plucky that one tends to forget her age. I hope I'm like her when I'm eighty."

And as Lélia was climbing out of the tub Louise advised her:

"You ought to take a cold shower, to get your blood going. I'm sure that would set you on your feet again."

The bedroom remained dark and silent for over an hour more. When finally Sophie glided into the studio, noiselessly, like a shadow, wearing her close-fitting trousers and her sweater, the pink-shaded lamp was burning beside the couch and all the usual points of light were shining in the night landscape of Paris.

She did not go to the kitchen, so Louise did not immediately realize that she was up. It was only on bringing back the metal ashtrays she had been polishing that Louise, with a start of surprise, discovered the girl there, motionless in the half-darkness.

"You didn't ring?"

"I didn't need anything."

"Mademoiselle Lélia has gone out. I whipped up some eggs for her in a glass of port, and it seemed to fix her up a bit. She was worried about her audition."

Louise would probably have offered Sophie the same remedy had she not noticed the bottle within reach of her hand.

"What will you have to eat?"

"Nothing just now."

"I hope you're not going out."

"I don't know."

Louise waited, knowing further questions would follow.

"Has my grandmother gone?"

"Where would she go, poor thing?"

"Is she in bed?"

"No. She's sitting in her armchair."

"Go and tell her I'd like to see her."

Louise went through the kitchen muttering to herself, more than ever convinced that employers are a race apart and that it's no use trying to understand them.

Sophie had lit a cigarette and was waiting, her eyes fixed on the door. She had time to smoke the cigarette to the end and light another, and she was about to stand up impatiently when at last the old woman glided into the darkest corner of the room, where she was merely a black-and-white figure.

She was wearing the same black dress as on the first day. She had probably just put it on, as though to pay a call, and she had changed out of her red slippers.

Without moving, Sophie said:

"I beg your pardon, Juliette."

It was the first time since they had agreed to do so that she had addressed her grandmother thus, and she hoped that the old woman would appreciate her intention.

"I ought perhaps to have gone into your room to say so. I thought it was better to talk to you here."

She was calm, clearheaded, and unmoved. She had been in the wrong, the previous night. She had shown unnecessary cruelty and she was anxious to admit it. That was all.

While she spoke, the old woman stepped forward into the ring of light, and Sophie noticed, to her surprise, that she had been drinking.

On her normally almost colorless face the cheekbones were flushed and the eyelids red-rimmed; her eyes had a suspect glitter; her walk was uncertain and wavering, as though she was moving in an insubstantial world.

"May I sit down?"

Her voice, too, was hesitant, and she dabbed at her nostrils with a handkerchief before speaking.

"You've no need to apologize to me. I haven't forgotten that I'm in your home. Do you understand? You're at home here, but as for me, even in what you call my room, I'm not at home."

She repeated words and fragments of sentences, intent on saying what she had decided to say. She must have thought about it all day, preparing the scene and seeking inspiration or courage from red wine.

"I'm used to it. You mustn't worry about me. The

habit of being in other people's homes, I mean. Really, I was only in my own home for a year and a half, after Adrien's death. Before that I wasn't in my own home but in my daughter's and son-in-law's. I wasn't even quite part of the family. I was something in between the dog and the servants."

There was a certain bitterness, but beyond that something sly about her smile, revealing a secret satisfaction with the role she was playing.

"Do you remember Dick, the dachshund? Even Dick always came to sniff at me as though I were a stranger when I went into the dining room or the living room."

"Do you really have to talk about all that?"

"Hush! You sent your maid to fetch me, and I've come. No offense taken. You're in your own home, as I said. I've been waiting ever since this morning for an opportunity to speak to you and I'm going to do so, even if you throw me out afterward."

"There's no question of my throwing you out."

"It would be the best thing to do, though, because, you see, we will never get on together, the pair of us. We understand one another too well. I was able to stay at your mother's for eight years because your mother and I have always been strangers to one another.

"I knew at once that we had nothing in common, when she was only a baby. People imagine that a mother loves her children automatically. They try to make one believe it. It's useful, isn't it? Only it isn't true."

"Listen, Grandmother . . ."

"You see! You've already given up calling me Juli-

107

ette, whereas I haven't told you one-tenth of the truth. You're afraid of the truth, but in your heart of hearts you know I'm right. Your mother doesn't love you either. She loved the twins, not you. You were only one-half of the twins and, from her point of view, the wrong half."

It was no good protesting or trying to stop her. She would go on to the end, unless she lost the thread of the speech she had prepared and in which it was not yet possible to distinguish candor from craft.

What was immediately clear was that she was not going away. Otherwise she would have taken advantage of Sophie's being asleep to leave the apartment, after sending for Pilou to remove her belongings.

Now she was strengthening her position, although some of the things she said were spontaneous and had a ring of truth, were, indeed, quite touching.

"What was I saying? I was talking about Boulevard Saint-Germain. While you were still small I was useful for looking after you when the servants were busy. When I became superfluous they tolerated me for fear of what people would say.

"With your grandfather Prédicant, whom you won't remember, when I lived on Boulevard Raspail, I wasn't in my own home either. I was his wife. In other words, I was in his house. I formed part of his property, somewhat like the printing press. So much so that when I wanted to go away, he prevented me."

"Did you intend to leave him?"

"I could hardly leave him, as you put it, unless I'd been really with him. Do you mind if I drink out of your glass?"

Then she went on:

"You've never married, and it's not for me to say whether you were right or wrong. That depends on you. We're all alike, it's true, and then we're all different. I myself was married three times, twice to the same man, and I only had my own home when I'd become a practically helpless old woman. And at that point they wanted to drive me out, to shut me up in a home, or perhaps force me to go and live like a tramp on the embankment. I'd have preferred that to the home. I did consider it. . . ."

She looked at the glass and bottle. "Sophie?"

"Yes?"

"Would you mind if I went to fetch some wine from my room?"

"Louise will bring you some."

"I'd rather go myself. But you've got to wait for me. You promise to wait?"

She wandered off unsteadily and stayed away longer than necessary. When she returned, she had regained her composure and she set down her bottle of wine and her glass beside the whisky.

Sophie's glass was empty.

"Can I give you some?"

The girl let her do so.

"I'd intended to tell the story of my life, so that you might know, so that somebody would know. Yesterday in bed I'd already begun writing notes on scraps of paper. I'd like to tell everything, particularly the things that are usually hidden, even though it might make you hate me.

"Mark my words, Sophie! Even if you've lived

through a good deal for your age, I've had more experience than you.

"Wait now! I'm losing the thread. I ought to begin with Moulins. I'll do so someday. It'll have to come out in the end. Today I've been drinking a little wine. When I came in, you thought I was tipsy.

"But I know what I'm saying and I'm telling you this: we're both of us women. Like it or not, you're a woman and so am I. Well, a woman . . . Look at your friend Lélia! Remember the women who were here last night. . . .

"A woman is never a complete being. That's what I was trying to say: a complete being. A woman is a piece of something, of something that perhaps doesn't exist. Do you hear? You'll think of that later on, and a long time after I'm dead you'll realize that I was right.

"A piece of something that doesn't exist!"

Pleased with herself, she glanced defiantly at Sophie as she drank.

"We all try to fasten on to something or other—all of us, you, me, Lélia, the others—we're like pieces of a puzzle, not knowing exactly what's missing. . . ."

At the most unexpected moment she suddenly burst into tears, perhaps because Sophie's gaze was too penetrating and apparently indifferent. She deliberately delayed wiping her eyes, to make sure her tears would be seen.

"I've been searching all my life. Then you came. . . ."

Sophie, increasingly hostile, could not conceal an expression of disgust. She had understood. Her

110

grandmother was following a plan, clumsily, like a bad actress, not knowing by what means to win her sympathy.

"You came ..." she repeated, searching for inspiration.

"I know."

"What do you know?"

"What you're going to say. You thought you'd found the answer at last, that with me, in my home, you would ..."

The old woman's eyes narrowed and darkened.

"Do you despise me?" she asked sharply.

"No."

"Do you hate me?"

"No."

"You merely put up with me here, don't you? Like the rest of the lame dogs you pick up in the street. Only I ... I ... I ..."

She had stopped acting. Something had snapped, and she collapsed, sobbing, in the armchair from which she had just risen.

"I can't stand it any more!" she screamed.

SIX

Involuntarily, with an instinctive gesture, and possibly in order to bring this painful scene to an end, Sophie began to stroke the old woman's head; and it was when her hand, parting the thin veil of hair, disclosed the pink skull, hard and shiny as an anatomical specimen, that she experienced a pang.

Juliette was very old and she was crying like a child, without hiding her face, a mute pathetic question in her eyes. Children, too, seem to be asking why they need to suffer.

"Calm down. You'll see...."

She went on saying "You'll see, you'll see..." without connecting the words to anything; but to the old woman they became a sort of promise to which she gradually clung.

"I shouldn't have done it," Sophie went on. "I don't know why, last night, I suddenly wanted to hurt you."

Juliette's sobs seemed to surge up from somewhere in the depths of her chest, rising slowly through her throat before breaking out at last. To be on a level with her grandmother, Sophie knelt down on the carpet and put her arm around the bony shoulders, which she now touched for the first time.

She had never been so close to the skinny neck, which was heaving spasmodically, and she felt a sense of physical repulsion mingled with pity.

"I'm cruel sometimes. . . ."

Juliette shook her head. "It's my fault," she gasped. She was still weeping, but with a slower rhythm, gradually recovering her breath.

The girl continued, knowing it was a mistake to talk so much but unable to keep silent:

"Perhaps it was because I'd been drinking. I beg your pardon."

"You don't . . . you don't have to beg my pardon."

She gently freed herself, and Sophie, though conscious of the absurdity of her posture, didn't dare alter it immediately.

"It's I who . . ."

A hiccup interrupted the old woman's words, and she apologized with a twisted attempt at a smile.

"It was I who tried to arouse your pity. . . . I . . . wanted you to take an interest in me. . . . I was jealous. . . ."

Instead of cutting short the scene by rising to her feet, Sophie chose to sit down on the carpet beside the armchair.

"Not only jealous of Lélia, you know. You mustn't tell her that. . . . Of all of them! . . . Perhaps of you

yourself, too . . . I wanted you to pity me and protect
me . . ."

Although still mournful, she had begun to make
fun of herself a little.

"If you knew how tired I am, Sophie! For so many
years I've tried so hard. . . ."

Her glance fell on the bottle of wine, with its
tempting glints, but she dared not make a request or
a gesture. Both of them were conscious of the fragile
nature of this lull, this respite, and neither felt strong
enough to renew the battle.

Juliette confessed with a wry laugh:

"I don't even know what I tried to do! And yet God
knows I wore myself out. I was wrong to tell you such
things. I won't do it again. You'll see! You won't even
notice that I'm in the house. You seemed so strong to
me. . . . You are strong, aren't you?"

Those words, and the exact intonation with which
they were uttered, were to linger in Sophie's memory.
At the time, she could not have said whether there
was irony in the old woman's voice and in her eyes,
which were now dry and glittering.

"You seemed so strong. . . . You are strong, aren't you?"

In spite of that "aren't you?" Juliette did not expect
an answer. She was really weary. Her features, usually
so clear-cut, had become limp. Her face was puffy,
and her body, huddled in the armchair, seemed
smaller and incredibly light.

"I'm going to put you to bed."

Sophie understood the look in her grandmother's
eyes and poured her a glass of wine.

"On condition you stop fretting." She put on a deliberately playful tone. "That you lie down immediately and go to sleep."

To avoid provoking a fresh scene through some tactless word or gesture, she pressed the electric bell, and Louise appeared at the door, a censorious expression on her face.

"Is my grandmother's bed ready?"

"I've only got to turn it down, mademoiselle. I took advantage of her being in here to air the room."

"Come along."

The whole situation was difficult and ambiguous. There was peace, but it was an uneasy and probably provisional peace, because mistrust and resentment had only been hidden under an emotion that had been aroused at the cost of some distress.

Sophie took Juliette to her bedroom but did not go in.

"I'll leave you to undress. Louise will help you. I'll come and say good night when you're in bed."

"You mustn't bother."

She went back, however, after Louise had carried in a tray with a little soup and some cheese.

"Sleep well."

"You, too."

The old woman avoided asking Sophie, as she usually did, whether she was going out. That was no longer any business of hers. Had she not promised to be discreet?

In the studio, Sophie was nibbling a slice of ham, without much appetite, when the telephone rang. It was one of last night's visitors.

"Did you find a bunch of keys this morning?"

She went to ask Louise.

"No, Pierre. The maid hasn't found anything but a couple of handkerchiefs and one glove."

"Not too tired?"

"Just a little."

"We're about to start out again. I don't know yet what it'll turn out like. Won't you come and join us?"

She was tempted. The stillness of the apartment was oppressive, and she was moving limply, like . . .

Telephone in hand, she mentally concluded: ". . . like a sick animal."

Was it because a short while ago Juliette had spoken of lame dogs?

"No, Pierre. I'm going to bed. I've made up my mind."

"Well, it's our loss. Sleep well."

She was trying to recover her grandmother's exact words, but could only remember the drift of them:

"Your mania for picking up lame dogs. . . ."

She hadn't used the word *mania*.

"Your need to . . ."

That was something more significant, more revealing. The old woman knew that Lélia had not been the first. She had managed to worm the story out of Louise.

One of her last remarks, this evening, had been:

"You are strong, aren't you? . . ."

Sophie, setting the two ideas side by side, felt ill at ease, practically certain now that the reference to her strength had been ironic. If she had really been strong, would she have felt the need to pick up . . .

With an abrupt movement she tossed her hair back,

116

furious at finding her thoughts tend that way, at being at the mercy of an ever-watchful old woman who claimed to be telling her the truth about herself.

For Juliette was spying on her, anxious to discover her weak points, as she had already started to do through the door on Rue de Jouy.

"You can clear up, Louise."

"You don't want any dessert?"

"No, thanks."

She flung herself down on the couch, the way a dog, still bristling with anger, rushes into its kennel.

"*. . . lame dogs . . .*"

Furious though she was, she could not repress a smile. It was disturbing. Just now she had thought of her scene with Juliette as a grotesque comedy, a collection of phrases intended to arouse her pity.

Now that she was alone, absorbed in self-analysis, trying to concentrate on some point in space amid the flickering lights, there emerged from the jumble of words and playacting a few isolated gleams, which she could not succeed in connecting with one another but which intrigued her.

What her grandmother had said about the twins, for instance, the twins, each of whom their mother thought of as being only part of a whole being.

Had this thought not occurred to her, too, less distinctly, and hadn't she seen herself as the worse half of that whole?

Juliette admitted to having wished for her own mother's death, particularly that evening when she went to get her father at the café. The same thing had happened to Sophie, and even before she was ten years old she had wished for the death of her father and her sister, Adrienne, into the bargain.

She'd be left on her own. In deep mourning, very upright, very grown up, she would lead the family's funeral procession while people turned around in the street to watch her pass.

"I had to wait till I was an old woman and Adrien was dead to have a nook of my own. . . ."

Sophie's curiosity was aroused, and she asked herself questions without finding answers that satisfied her. She had thought she knew the old woman, had seen her as a complex being indeed, but one whose mind she could follow, whose reactions she could foresee.

And now that they had been living under the same roof for almost a week, she realized that her grandmother had learned more about her than she had learned about the old woman.

She had hated her. She had almost pitied her.

Now her dominant feeling was curiosity, not only about Juliette but also about what Juliette thought of her.

The old woman frightened her, somewhat like those gypsies who stop you in the street and take your hand to read your fortune, while you smile uneasily.

The sounds of washing up had ceased in the kitchen. The light had gone out under the door. Sophie stayed for a long while, smoking cigarettes, without once reaching for a drink. At last she rose and made her way quietly to the back entrance to listen at her grandmother's door.

She heard nothing. The light was on in Louise's room, where the maid was undressing. So the two women could not have been together, as Sophie had pictured them, quietly gossiping in the overheated bedroom where the stove was purring.

She felt ashamed of what she was doing. She refused to become jealous herself. But then why was she here?

She went back to her room, undressed, and swallowed two sleeping pills. She wanted to sleep, to stop thinking about Juliette or about herself.

Her grandmother had declared that they were alike!

She switched off the light, and for a few minutes longer she struggled against thoughts which became increasingly hazy and ended in confusion.

When, much later, Lélia came home and talked to her at some length excitedly, she made replies and even asked questions, of which she remembered nothing when she woke next morning.

It was early, barely ten o'clock. She looked at her sleeping friend and thought about her "lame dogs" with a detachment far removed from the previous night's emotion.

Today she felt no need of alcohol when she woke, but took a long bath after visiting Louise in the kitchen to order her breakfast.

"Is my grandmother up?"

"She's done her room already."

And when Sophie frowned at this, she explained.

"She insisted on that, right from the start. When I try to help her, she gets angry. But I'm beginning to suspect that she's not as strong as she makes out. This morning she made me think that she was a really decrepit old lady."

Sophie lay for half an hour in the warm water, reading the morning papers. Then she had breakfast in the studio, where there was the same pale, sharp sunlight that she had missed the day before. She considered taking her car and driving at top speed along the highways for an hour or two, as she often liked to do.

Finally, rather reluctantly, she went to knock at the old lady's door.

"Come in."

Juliette was sitting in her armchair, not reading, doing nothing. Was she waiting, perhaps? The radio was silent, and there was no wine on either of the tables.

She started to rise and give up her seat, but Sophie perched astride the other chair.

"Do you allow smoking?"

"I've always been surrounded by smokers and it's never bothered me."

Whereas the girl seemed fresher than the day before, Juliette, although not quite in the lamentable state described by Louise, nonetheless suddenly looked her full age.

"Did I talk a lot of nonsense yesterday?"

"Don't you remember what you said?"

For once the old woman spoke frankly, with a smile.

"Yes! Not every detail, perhaps. But the general drift. Did you used to be shocked to see me drinking?"

Sophie, trying to recall Boulevard Saint-Germain, did not remember having seen her grandmother drink or having heard any reference to the subject.

"How old was I when I left? In 1944, I was sixty-five. Believe it or not, I'd never been drunk in my life. It was with Adrien that I took to it. During our first marriage he didn't drink either.

"When I went back to him, he was known in all the local bistros, and they used to pour out his glass of red wine before he asked for it. In the evenings I'd go in search of him, and I began to be well known, too. They'd tell me what time he'd been in and in which direction he'd gone off. Little by little I took to imitating him."

She was almost merry. Although wearing her dressing gown and slippers, she had done her hair carefully and tied a bright scarf around her shriveled neck.

"Did you sleep well?"

"I took a sleeping pill," Sophie admitted. "I didn't even hear Lélia come in."

"Is she still in bed?"

"Unless she made some appointment last night, she has no engagement today. I've asked Louise to serve lunch for three at half past one."

Having come to the end of small talk, they fell silent, both staring at the copper kettle, whose quivering contents and gleaming surface made it the focal point of the room. Sophie wondered what her grandmother did with all that boiling water. Did she pour it down the sink for the pleasure of making a fresh kettleful sing, or did she from time to time let it grow cool?

She was determined not to speak first. Before coming in she had resolved to leave the initiative to Juliette, and subsequently not to say anything that might scare her.

She waited, with a touch of impatience, convinced that the old woman would finally talk, and wondering how she would begin.

"I know what you're thinking."

"What am I thinking?" Sophie retorted.

"You're saying to yourself that I'm dying to tell my life story and that I don't know how to go about it. Admit it!"

"It was something of the sort."

"Would it interest you to learn what a really quite ordinary woman did during eighty years of life?"

"You say I'm like you."

"I said so yesterday because I was tipsy."

"Are you sure you were as tipsy as all that?"

"Tipsy enough to exaggerate. Doesn't it happen to you, when you've been drinking, to feel sorry for yourself and to be convinced that the whole world is in league against you?"

Sophie preferred not to reply.

"Basically," the old woman went on, "I don't pity myself. Or else one would have to pity everyone, and life would no longer be possible."

The girl noted mentally, as though the words might someday provide a key:

"*. . . and life would no longer be possible . . .*"

She had been quite right to think that the old woman was less simple than she had originally thought.

"Have you never felt pity?" She could not resist

pressing the point, although she had vowed to herself not to intervene.

And Juliette replied with a cruel smile:

"I didn't even feel pity for my poor old Adrien."

For a moment she seemed to be following her thought through space.

"There's one thing I want to tell you, because I'd like to know if you've had the same experience. It may seem strange, but I've never met anyone to whom I could put the question."

"What question?"

"Wait. In order for you to understand, I shall have to tell the story. You're not in a hurry, or impatient?"

"I've nothing to do today."

"Do you really not want the armchair? Suppose you lie down on the bed. In your studio you're always stretched out on the couch."

Did she suspect the repugnance that her granddaughter felt for a bed still almost warm from an old woman's body? In any case, she did not press her.

"I've told you about Moulins, about my parents, about Gaston Demarie, the son of the piano-store owner, and of what went on in the shed. Later on, when I heard men talking about that sort of thing, I was surprised that they thought it so important. I told Adrien frankly about my experiences, and it made him unhappy for a long time.

"I suppose, being a woman, you understand. Even when, eventually—and heaven knows it took a long time!—when at last, as I say, I began to enjoy it, that didn't make any bond between me and that fool with the mustache.

"You see what I mean? Even when he was doing what he liked with certain parts of my body, and even when I was proving as compliant as he could wish, I hadn't any sense of giving him any part of my real self.

"I still considered myself pure and untouched, in spite of my terror at the thought of certain possible consequences. If I never looked for similar pleasure elsewhere, I would no doubt have accepted any opportunities that might have presented themselves.

"Don't think I'm talking nonsense. I need to stress the point in order to explain the sequel. I didn't like my parents' home, as I told you, and I found that quite natural, since it had not been set up for me but for them. They were in their own place. I was only a transient visitor, waiting till I was old enough to begin my own life.

"If only parents would understand that! But I'm coming to the nub of the matter. I met Adrien when I was twenty-two and wondering whether I would ever escape from Moulins. He was three years older than me and had only recently come to that town. He said he was a journalist; I'll tell you about that later on. A senator from Allier, who published a little paper at Moulins, had signed him on in Paris on a friend's recommendation. I promptly fell in love with him, as fully and sincerely as anyone could."

She cast a stealthy glance to make sure the girl was listening.

"Am I boring you?"

"No."

"You saw that couple the other evening, under the

124

archway. For months on end, Adrien and I were like that couple, in the freezing darkness of back streets, where my hands became blue with cold and I had to interrupt his kisses to blow my nose. He confided in me his hatred of provincial life, his eagerness to get back to Paris and to take me there. And then one day he announced that he had a job waiting for him there, on a leading newspaper.

"When I went home, I had the taste of his saliva in my mouth, and my lips were chapped with cold.

"I introduced him to my parents. He took to coming in the evenings, twice a week at first, then three times, then five times a week, to sit in the room at the back of the shop, where my mother sat knitting under the oil lamp and pretended not to pay attention to us, while my father went to the café to play cards.

"We loved one another. Our marriage was a real marriage, although we didn't have a church wedding because my father was what was called an atheist. There was much talk about the separation of church and state, and it was even proposed to drive the monks and nuns from their convents. At Moulins, on account of the Sisters of the Visitation, the Carmelites, and the Augustinian Canonesses, the infantrymen of the garrison were on the alert, and fights broke out in the streets, although they were not as serious as in certain Breton villages.

"Some twenty guests came to our wedding breakfast, which took place in the banqueting hall of the Hôtel du Dauphin."

"The hotel still exists. I've eaten there when passing through."

"We took the night train, Adrien and I, leaving the others to eat and drink. At seven o'clock that evening we had settled down, not in a sleeping car, but in a second-class carriage where, by good luck, there were no other travelers.

"I can still picture us side by side on a seat facing the engine.

"I had just fulfilled my childhood and girlhood dream, the dream of every woman. I had got married that very morning. Nobody henceforward could do anything to change that. I had a gold ring on my finger. Adrien, wearing a new suit, had his arm around my waist, and my head lay on his shoulder.

"I loved him, I repeat. I was excited. And while the train sped on, tossing us about, and Adrien was kissing me, I was staring straight in front of me.

"At that precise moment I was making a discovery that was to leave its mark on my life, although I did not know this until later. That evening I thought it was emotion, and panic at leaving my familiar surroundings and venturing into a new world of which I had only a vague notion.

"I was not sad, or, strictly speaking, frightened.

"Adrien was worried, and asked me: 'Are you cold?'

" 'No. Nothing's the matter.'

" 'It's probably the movement of the train.'

"Surely men ought to feel the same thing? What I was discovering, Sophie, was that I was going to live, in fact was already living, with a stranger.

"My head lay against his chest. I remember I could feel his wallet in his pocket. I knew his smell and the texture of his flesh, although he had never fully possessed me. He hadn't tried to. He didn't know, at the time, about my experiences with Gaston in the annex.

"That's not what matters. When it did take place, a little later, it altered nothing.

"What I want to stress is that I loved him, that I had become his wife a few hours ago, and yet I already knew that I was bound to a being whom I would never know and who would never know me either.

"We would share the same home and sleep in the same bed, we might perhaps have children, we would talk and laugh and quarrel and cry, but nevertheless we'd remain strangers to one another forever.

"Do you think I'm ridiculous?"

Sophie merely murmured:

"I'd never thought of things that way."

"Are you sure of that? Isn't it for that reason that you dislike the idea of finding a man, a stranger, in your bed in the morning? As far as I'm concerned, I was not mistaken, and the feeling I had in the train that night has been with me all my life. I still felt it when Adrien died a year and a half ago.

"Is there something abnormal about me? I first lived with Adrien for seven years on Rue de Jouy, in the very place where you came to fetch me, and the furniture you see here was all bought, piece by piece, as was the stove, during that period.

"We were very poor. Or, rather, we sometimes had money for a little while and then none at all.

"Adrien hadn't completely lied to me. He did small jobs for the newspapers, but he had no secure situation, and I soon realized that he never would.

"He was the sort of man who tells stories to himself

and to other people. Sometimes he was taken seriously and would get a regular wage, and we were flush for a while.

"Then it would be discovered that he had lied, that there was no substance in him. He would not lose heart, but would throw himself into a fresh venture. There was a time, for instance, when he tried to start a revolutionary sort of weekly, and he even found the money to rent an office and order printed stationery.

"It was an odd sort of life. When we hadn't a penny left in the house, he would write to Peter or Paul to borrow money, and he'd send me to take the letter. Some men used to misunderstand, and took my presence for a scarcely concealed invitation.

"Sometimes I let them have what they wanted. I don't know if Adrien suspected. I've even wondered whether the people who misunderstood his intentions this way were really mistaken.

"In the train, I suspected nothing of all this. And yet I knew."

She looked Sophie straight in the eyes.

"Do *you* believe that there's such a thing as a real couple, made up of a man and a woman who are not strangers to one another?"

The girl gave a nervous laugh.

"I've never tried."

"Because you don't believe in it! The position's the same in the case of two men or two women, relatives or friends. I may be your grandmother, but I'm as much a stranger to you, if not more so, as the girl who's now asleep in your bedroom.

"That's what I wanted to say to you, quietly, without our losing our tempers. I don't know why I set about it so badly yesterday. Or, rather, I do know. Adrien spent his life telling stories that he came to believe in the end. I wonder if all of us don't do much the same thing.

"I told you I loved him. I believed I did. There are times when I still believe I did, when I tell myself that's what they call 'love.'

"I realize, when I think about it, that I chiefly needed something solid to cling to. I was incapable of living alone. I felt alone in my parents' home.

"I thought he was going to be a support to me, that together we would form . . . Actually, what should we have formed? Do you know? Does anyone know?

"Guess what he told me, one night when he was dead drunk, a few months before his death. . . . Don't try! It's so funny that I burst out laughing, while he stared at me without understanding. He told me, positively, that I had ruined his life, that he had always needed a woman who would take him in hand, prevent him from making a fool of himself, someone reliable and reassuring. He added that when he met me I seemed so calm and self-confident that he believed I was such a woman.

"Do you see the joke? I married him to have someone to support me because I thought he was dependable, while he, aware of his own weakness, was counting on me to protect him!"

She tried to meet Sophie's eyes to note her reaction, but the girl went on silently staring at the stove.

"I'll tell you, moreover . . ."

Louise knocked on the door to announce lunch.

"Is Lélia up?"

"I woke her half an hour ago, and she's just finished her bath."

Lélia was waiting for them in the studio, anxiously trying to guess from the attitude of the two women what had been going on. She did not fail to observe the old lady's satisfaction and Sophie's uneasy, serious self-absorption, which boded no good.

Sophie, however, remembered to ask her:

"How did your audition go?"

"Have you forgotten?"

"Forgotten what?"

"I talked to you about it last night for a quarter of an hour, and you even asked me questions."

"What questions?"

"I don't remember. Weren't you awake?"

"I'd taken a sleeping pill."

The three of them sat down, Sophie in the middle, and passed the hors d'oeuvres almost ceremoniously. Louise had put a bottle of Saint-Emilion in front of the old woman's place, as well as the white Alsatian wine.

"They're hiring me, but not until next year, and on condition that I find some new songs. The director thinks as you do, that my repertoire is all right for a nightclub or for television but that it wouldn't get across in a popular music hall. I'll have to start looking for something."

The person who was most surprised was Louise, who could not understand the peaceable, relaxed mood of the three women, or the smiling courtesy they showed one another.

"Do have some more prawns, Juliette."

Sophie had been careful not to say "grandmother," and this was acknowledged by a grateful glance.

Lélia still knew nothing, except that the other two had spent part of the morning in tête-à-tête in the old woman's room. Her instinct told her that Juliette's self-assurance implied a danger to herself.

She was almost as tactless as when she had been annoyed with Sophie on the evening of the party, but this time it was on purpose, out of resentment.

Pretending to read the label on the bottle of red wine, she commented, as though Louise had made a mistake:

"I thought you preferred your own."

Juliette was not fooled. She merely replied:

"This one is excellent. It's a much better wine, in fact, but I couldn't have afforded it and I'm only afraid of becoming used to it."

Peace still prevailed, at any rate on the surface.

"You are strong, aren't you? . . ."

In Sophie's mind that remark was associated with others and conferred a new meaning on them. Isolated phrases, casually dropped in their conversations, were beginning to come together, though there were still gaps.

It was too soon to reconstruct or understand everything, but one thing was now certain: Juliette Viou was dangerous.

SEVEN

It was snowing. Sophie, reading a novel, glanced from time to time over the top of her book at the flakes, which were falling ever more thickly and slowly and beginning to lie on rooftops and parked cars. As for Lélia, after considering putting on a record, she had thought it wiser not to do so, and she was sitting cross-legged on the floor, with magazines scattered around her, like a child amid its toys.

The bay window, although draft-proof, let in cold air, which spread in waves through the warmth from the radiators. The two women, apparently calm but really tense, kept silent, each of them waiting for the opportunity to make peace.

They had not quarreled, and that was what made reconciliation difficult. They had dined with friends at Fouquet's the previous evening, and Lélia had only had to cross the Champs-Elysées to reach her nightclub. The evening had started quietly for both of them. Sophie had gone with her companions to the Elysée Club, where she had sat chatting at several tables without, however, joining any party, and at about half past two she had drawn her red car up outside La Patate.

She thought, without being certain of it, that she saw a figure disappear into the darkness, but she thought no more about it. She had asked no questions of the doorman who greeted her. On entering the dimly lit room she had looked around for her friend and had been annoyed to see her sitting at a table with two noisy Americans and a little Japanese hostess.

Their eyes had met. Sophie, with assumed indifference, had sat down by herself at the bar.

And that was really all. As she sipped her drink she heard loud voices and laughter from the Americans' table, but she avoided looking at it, and sat mechanically tearing a booklet of matches into shreds.

Ten or fifteen minutes went by, and then she had suddenly paid for her drink, to the barman's surprise, and left in a fit of resentment.

She had not gone anywhere else. Back on Quai de Bourbon she had gone straight to bed, and she had barely switched off the light when the front door opened and closed again. Lélia had not put on the light, but had undressed in the darkness, and once in bed had leaned over hesitantly toward her friend's bed.

"Are you angry?" she whispered. "They wouldn't let me go, and I was afraid of their turning nasty when they were drunk. François had the same thought and was signaling to me to be patient."

Receiving no reply, she tried another method, and slipped in beside Sophie, nestling her head against her friend's shoulder and whispering in her ear:

"I promise you I won't do it again."

It was unwise of her to seek warmth and consolation in Sophie's bed, unwise to lay her head where she had. She could not know this, because she had not heard Juliette tell about that scene in the train, when a different head had been laid against a different shoulder.

"I discovered that I had a stranger beside me and that I was going to live with a stranger."

The exact words didn't matter. Lélia, too, was a stranger to Sophie, so remote from her at that moment that she did not feel impelled to answer her. And that went not for Lélia alone but for all the other women who had preceded her and who would follow her.

Each of the girls could hear her companion breathing, was aware of her heartbeats, and was sad, for different reasons and with different thoughts, which they could not communicate to one another.

It was beginning to feel colder, even in the apartment. Perhaps it was at that moment that the snow began to fall? Lélia crept back into her own bed, and, without seeing her, Sophie knew that her eyes remained wide open in the darkness.

They had got up early and had not talked. They had listened to the radio as they ate. Sophie had not asked Louise for news of Juliette, and the maid had deliberately said nothing.

In the apartment that morning each of the women

seemed to be immured in silence. And suddenly, as Lélia, who could stand it no longer, was just about to speak, only waiting to see her friend's eyes reach the end of a chapter, the front doorbell made them both start.

They heard the maid go to the door and say a brief word. When she came back she merely held out a calling card to Sophie.

JOSEPH CHARON
POLICE SUPERINTENDENT

The name was followed by a tiny reproduction of the Legion of Honor and of what looked like two other decorations.

"Ask him to come in."

Lélia sprang up and made for the bedroom; the Superintendent only caught a glimpse of her figure. As he came toward the couch he had to step aside to avoid treading on magazines.

"I hope I'm not disturbing you."

He glanced at his watch, which he had already consulted downstairs.

"It's half past eleven," he stated.

"I know. Please sit down."

"I don't want you to think that I've delayed my visit. In the past few days I've twice called on your concierge and each time she's warned me not to disturb you."

He gave a knowingly sympathetic smile.

"First of all I wanted to thank you for the very great service you did me. To be quite frank with you, I realize that when I came to ask for your assistance I did

135

not envisage the consequences that your co-operation might entail for you. When I became aware of these, I was seized with remorse. Doubtless owing to my professional mentality, I had seen the problem at first only from the administrative point of view. . . ."

As he spoke, he seemed to be looking around him for some trace of the old woman whom he had seen, to his great relief, leaving the condemned house on Rue de Jouy in the company of her granddaughter.

"My visit, then, has a double purpose: to thank you and to set my conscience at rest. I hope I haven't created too many problems for you."

Smiling politely but coolly, Sophie murmured:

"Not too many, no."

"Is the person in question here?"

Her eyelids flickered. Then, looking at each of the doors in turn, he asked in a lower voice:

"May I speak?"

Why not? Louise had probably warned the old woman, who must now be in the kitchen with her ear glued to the door. Well, so much the worse for her!

"May I make bold to ask how you've settled things?"

She almost replied, "Nothing's settled." For in fact that was the truth. But what was the good of discussing it? She merely said:

"I had a spare room in my apartment, and my grandmother is occupying it."

"I saw that she had removed part of her furniture and I took the precaution of having the rest stored in a nearby warehouse."

He gave an embarrassed little cough.

"I happened to meet the doctor who questioned her through the door, and who is a friend of mine. He was curious to know what had become of her, and how she's behaving now. I gathered that he failed to form a final opinion. May I ask whether you have one?"

"Do you want me to tell you if I think my grandmother is mad?"

"I wouldn't have gone as far as that. As I explained to you the other morning, in a case of this sort the authorities are practically powerless, and I sought the only solution that's available to us when the situation demands it. The fact that the doctor has since shown himself anxious, if not skeptical . . ."

She rose to pour a drink, without inquiring of her visitor what he wanted, knowing that it would be whisky.

"Apart from the thanks I owe you as a man and as a policeman, my visit is entirely unofficial. You are a famous woman and your active life and the risks that you run are well known. I would not like to be responsible for . . ."

"Your good health, Superintendent."

"Am I to understand that everything is going well and that you are not at all worried about your grandmother?"

What could she reply?

"I think she's satisfied to be here."

He did not ask her whether she herself was equally satisfied, but the question could be read in his eyes. Failing to elicit any reassuring answer, he clumsily concluded the message he had undertaken to bring.

"I told you the doctor was a friend of mine. I'm giving you his card, just in case. As you see, he lives on Place des Vosges, close by. He's a conscientious doctor, a real perfectionist, who doesn't stop worrying about his patients after he's lost sight of them. If at any time you should decide that a visit from him might be helpful, he'll be at your disposal, and if need be, since the lady in question has not seen him, you could pass him off as one of your acquaintances."

"That's very kind of him," she said, almost without irony. "Please thank him for me."

"Does she seem to you normal?"

"It depends on what you call normal, doesn't it? Can I swear that *I* am normal?"

He laughed. "Once more, your good health and many thanks. I won't bother you any longer. For some days now I'd had it on my conscience. When my wife advised me to . . ."

It was almost comic. He had given himself away and did not know how to put things right. Hadn't he admitted that he, a superintendent of police, kept his wife informed of his cases and possibly asked her advice about them?

Sophie would have liked to know what Madame Charon thought about Juliette, but her visitor, with profuse apologies, was now beating a retreat.

Hardly had the landing door closed behind him when the old woman emerged from the kitchen, distressed and suspicious.

"Did you hear?" Sophie asked her.

"Nearly everything. What are you going to do? Did you know I was listening?"

"I guessed you were. I was sure Louise would have warned you."

"Was it because I was behind the door that you didn't tell him anything?"

Sophie took her time, as though weighing the pros and cons, before replying:

"I had nothing to tell him."

"You don't believe I'm crazy, do you?"

"If you are . . ."

"But I'm not, Sophie, I swear it! I'm in my right mind! What makes me look odd to certain people is that I say what I think, what other people don't admit, what they persist in hiding even from themselves. If you'd rather, I'll hold my tongue. You won't send me to the home, will you? Where's that doctor's card? What's his name?"

Sophie read out the card in an undertone: "Dr. Paul Barbanel, 21 Place des Vosges," and handed it to her grandmother, who glared angrily at it, started to tear it up, and finally laid it on the marble mantelpiece.

"He never saw me. He never examined me. He merely asked me a dozen questions, no more, through the door. The proof that I'm not crazy is that they dared do nothing further and came to fetch you."

"Sit down."

"Are you still in doubt?"

"No. Sit down."

The old woman sat in an armchair, as wary as though she were facing an examining magistrate or Dr. Barbanel himself.

Instead of lying down on the couch as usual, Sophie seated herself in another chair, opposite her grandmother, thus increasing the latter's nervousness.

It seemed as though Juliette expected to be formally questioned, because she began by joking, with a forced laugh:

"I swear to tell the truth, the whole truth, and nothing but . . ."

She broke off to ask, in a more serious tone:

"What do you want to know? Tell me frankly. I'll answer you just as frankly, and I promise I won't lie."

"I don't suppose you have ever lied."

She was on dangerous ground here, and thought it wiser to make the somewhat ambiguous reply: "Sometimes."

"Your lies aren't real lies. You say nothing without a special reason for saying it. You sometimes talk about other people, but not very much. You talk chiefly about yourself."

"Do you know anyone who doesn't?"

"There's one side of you that escapes me. . . ."

"Me, too."

"Would you mind not interrupting me?"

"I'm sorry."

This was different from the interview in the room with the stove and the copper kettle, and even more different from the emotional outbursts of a certain other conversation. Partly, perhaps, because of the light of a snowy day, Sophie's face had never seemed so clear-cut, so implacable.

"So far you've told me practically nothing about

my grandfather. How did you come to know him?"

The grandchild was calling her grandmother to account, and the old woman made no protest.

"Do you want all the details?"

"All those that are important."

"That depends on the angle one's looking from, doesn't it?"

She remained quick-witted, able to follow a complicated train of thought.

"I told you about my life with Adrien, in broad strokes, but you can form only an incomplete picture of it. It all happened in another world, before the 1914 war, when buses were horse-drawn and the only noise in the streets was the rattle of cabs on the wooden roadway. I haven't kept any photographs, because they make me feel I'm looking at corpses."

She was not speaking the truth. On Rue de Jouy there had been at least one photograph, on the cherrywood chest. Whose portrait, Adrien Viou's? Prédicant's? Or someone else's? Had Juliette destroyed it, and if so, why?

"Picture Adrien in a frock coat and a top hat, then later wearing a bowler or a broad-brimmed boater."

"I'm not interested in what he wore."

"Just as you like. I told you we had ups and downs. In the spring of 1908 we were both wearing new clothes, since Adrien was at that time a sort of secretary to a public-works contractor who had become a deputy, and who was being accused of misappropriation. In order to defend himself and hit back at his enemies he proposed to found a newspaper.

"One day in May, Adrien took me to the Café de

Paris, the fashionable restaurant, where we were to lunch with this man and two others whose agreement was necessary.

"One of the two was named Gilbert Prédicant, and he owned a large printing plant on Avenue de Châtillon.

"Prédicant was tall and broad-shouldered, a handsome man of nearly forty, and during the meal he seemed more interested in me than in the explanations being provided by the other two.

"May I be frank? You won't tell me again that I'm always talking about myself?"

Sophie merely nodded.

"At thirty, I was still pretty, prettier than I'd been at twenty, with a calm and yet lively prettiness, and, in particular, as anyone who knew me at the time would have told you, I was one of those women whom men find intriguing. I won't say I didn't do it on purpose. I had a way of looking at them and listening to them that forced them to ask me sooner or later:

" 'What do you think?'

"To which I would reply by another question:

" 'About whom?'

" 'About me, for instance.'

"For men, just like women, as I had discovered, are all anxious to know what one thinks of them. They always seem to dread being seen otherwise than as they would like to be seen, or would like to see themselves.

"I suppose you don't want to hear about all the different stages we had to go through. One week later I got into a motorcar for the first time in my life, to go and lunch with Prédicant in a private room in a restaurant at Saint-Cloud.

"He was a bachelor. He had affairs, but he was not what was called a womanizer, and he spent most of his evenings at his club.

"After several weeks of more or less clandestine meetings, I told the whole thing to Adrien, who already suspected the truth.

"He asked me calmly:

" 'Where's it going to lead you?'

" 'He's begging me to leave you.'

" 'And get a divorce?'

" 'Not yet. He'll come to that later.'

" 'Are you in love?'

" 'Maybe.'

"That was true. Prédicant was a strong character, and I ran no risk of having to be a mother figure to him.

"For a whole year I lived in an apartment on Chaussée-d'Antin, which he'd had furnished for me. The hardest part was moving from the position of a kept woman to that of a wife.

"I managed that. As it happened, Adrien and I had not been married in church, which allowed me to become Madame Prédicant to the sound of organ music.

"Am I shocking you?"

"No."

It was not so much what Juliette was saying that interested Sophie as what she could guess behind the words.

"For years Adrien had led me to believe that it was

my fault that we hadn't had any children. With Prédicant, we'd no sooner stopped taking precautions than
I found myself pregnant.

"I had become an important, well-respected bour-
geoise. We had a double apartment, which was practically a private mansion, on Boulevard Raspail, and
for the summer a house with its own grounds near
Trouville.

"Just as my father, at Moulins, used to go and play
cards at the Brasserie de Paris, Prédicant would
spend his evenings at his club, when we weren't dining in town or going to the theater.

"Your mother was born. Although he was disappointed at having a daughter, he gave me the set of
jewelry of which you know the earrings and the rest
of which you may perhaps remember having seen
when you were small."

"Why did you want to leave him?"

Juliette did not answer right away. The question
took her by surprise, and she was honestly trying to
be as accurate as possible.

She began by asking a question.

"Do you feel that you're in a real, substantial
world, with solid walls and real things around you?"

A frown clouded Sophie's brow.

"Don't be annoyed! I'm trying to help you to understand. With Adrien I was less conscious of it, because we were both drifting like a couple of corks
tossed about in the eddies of Parisian life.

"With Prédicant I still drifted, but I drifted alone.
He stood solidly on his two feet, on his long legs. He
felt at home on Boulevard Raspail, and even more in

144

the printing plant on Avenue de Châtillon. He felt at home everywhere, in the Café de Paris, at his club, in the Bois, and at the theater. And things were real to him; our daughter was real, and so were the modern presses he sent for from America and the new buildings he put up at Montrouge.

"I could talk to you about Monotype, platen presses, and Lambert presses, and I know by heart the story of Ottmar Mergenthaler and Linotype. You see, age hasn't affected my memory! His father had daringly imported Linotype presses in 1890, when nobody believed in them, and they made his fortune."

"You were bored," Sophie muttered as though to herself.

"I hadn't time to be bored. I entertained—I had my at-home day and we gave dinner parties. We went out a great deal. Your mother was two and a half when the war broke out. Prédicant was not called up because he printed newspapers, which were considered indispensable for keeping up the nation's morale."

"And Adrien?"

"I never saw him. Prédicant wouldn't have allowed that. There had been a number of interviews between them, about which he never talked to me, on the subject of divorce, I suppose, and when, much later, I went back to live with Adrien, I didn't ask him whether he had got Prédicant to pay him.

"I know he was a uniformed orderly in some ministry before entering the censorship department."

Sophie reverted to her question.

"Did you decide to leave?"

"Not at that point. Several years after the war. And it's not quite true that I decided to. We were living in a new world. Women had cut their hair short and wore much the same kind of dresses that you're redis-covering today.

"Since I was a child I'd longed to be of some conse-quence, to be somebody, and I was of no more conse-quence on Boulevard Raspail than in my parents' home, or, later, in your parents'. Prédicant still hoped for a son, never suspecting that I took good care not to have one. I even had two miscarriages.

"Having your mother was enough for me. She's a real Prédicant, and the poor fellow ought to have been grateful to me, because a son would probably have taken after me.

"I had lovers, less from a need for sex than because I kept hoping for something different. I was over for-ty. Men of my own age were no longer interested in me. I was forced to hunt elsewhere, preferably among . . . Does this embarrass you."

"Not in the least."

"I used to choose the masculine equivalent of . . ." with a jerk of her chin, she indicated the bedroom where Lélia, impatient and resentful, had started singing.

"It was the time when Montparnasse was teeming with ambitious young men, and I sometimes used to run into Adrien. For a while he was a picture dealer there. He introduced me to painters who were still poor.

"Eventually Prédicant discovered everything, and it was then that I told him I wanted to leave him. I had no money, because we'd been married under the separate-property system. Nevertheless, old as I was, I was ready to plunge into the world of the Dôme, the Rotonde, and the small nightclubs that were springing up everywhere and were frequented by a few women my own age.

"I didn't mind not seeing my daughter any more. I said to myself that a few years spent really living were better than a long-drawn-out existence in an uncongenial home.

"Prédicant refused to give me my liberty, not because he needed me, but because his set did not tolerate divorce. When I insisted, threatening to run away as soon as I found the door open, he drew a paper from his wallet, a list of my lovers, of my rendezvous, descriptions of certain parties, certain wild nights spent among artists, and even a note of the sums of money I had sometimes given my companions.

"For the first time, in 1928, I heard the suggestion of a mental home. Not of Sainte-Anne's Hospital yet. What Prédicant threatened me with was an indefinite stay in some out-of-the-way nursing home.

"I knew he'd made up his mind, and I stood no chance of appeal, particularly since he could rely on official backing.

"Your mother was grown up by then. I was present at her wedding in 1930. She married a youngish publisher who had inherited a business founded by his grandfather and who seemed determined to be a success.

"Prédicant and I never spoke to one another except in public. If I could have killed him with the certainty of not getting caught, I believe I'd have done so, but he died a natural death in 1936.

"He hadn't even been ill. He collapsed in the street, quite suddenly, surrounded by fruit and vegetable carts.

"That's a story your parents never told you, or else they told it differently. To you and your sister, I was just an old woman at the end of the dinner table, and in the evenings sitting still and silent in a corner of the living room.

"I was fifty-seven when Prédicant died. Your mother inherited everything, printing plant, buildings, money. You're well off, since you've had your share of your father's legacy. The day you inherit from your mother and come into the Prédicant fortune you'll be an extremely rich woman. Do you hear? Extremely rich!"

A sly smile on the old woman's lips betrayed, for the first time, an unpleasant vulgarity.

"After all, even if I didn't make that money, it was through me that it came into your family, that it went to your mother and that you and your sister will enjoy it someday. I don't miss it. I don't want it. If I'd been different, if I'd gone about things in another way, it would have been entirely in my power to get possession of it.

"What could I do, penniless and nearly sixty? Montparnasse was a thing of the past, and the best I could hope for was to sell flowers outside cafés.

"I was convinced I would not live long. That's why, when your mother offered me a room on Boulevard Saint-Germain, I finally accepted.

"I knew she was not acting out of charity or out of pity, still less out of affection. If she was afraid of seeing me at liberty, just as her father had been afraid to let me leave him, it was because both of them had the same horror of scandal."

She averted her eyes for fear they might betray a sudden thought, a comparison with the present situation.

"I don't hold it against them. Your mother, like Prédicant, belongs to a society that has its laws and its principles. I suppose that allows one to live in peace with others and with oneself. With others, surely. But with oneself? Do *you* believe your mother lives in peace?"

What was the use of replying? Both knew the answer was no, and the old woman took care not to ask the same question about Sophie herself.

Silence fell. Lélia kept on singing, obstinately pacing to and fro in the bedroom.

"Was that what you wanted to know?"

She asked that like a schoolgirl at the blackboard.

"Can you still have doubts as to my sanity? Didn't I behave correctly on Boulevard Saint-Germain, paying for my keep by my discretion and dignity?

"There was one person in the family toward whom I still feel grateful. That was your father. I've no idea what he knew about my life. I'd be surprised if your mother told it all, even to him. Nonetheless he guessed a good part of it and he always watched me with friendly curiosity.

"In front of his wife he dared not pay too much attention to me or spoil me. He'd merely give me a knowing glance from time to time, and he would occasionally slip into my room unknown to your mother to leave some little present on my chest of drawers, some treat—for instance, during the war, a bar of chocolate or a currant bun."

Sophie showed some surprise.

"I'm convinced," the old woman went on, "that he, too, was looking for something he found neither in his wife nor in you girls, except possibly when you were small. He died when he was forty-seven.

"You see, it has sometimes struck me that if your father and I had belonged to the same generation and had been lucky enough to meet . . ."

She laughed.

"Make me hold my tongue, Sophie! Otherwise I shall end by letting you believe I was in love with your father."

Sophie did not laugh, did not smile, but rising suddenly went to open the bedroom door.

"Shut up, you!" she called out to Lélia.

She slammed the door. For the first time since Juliette had begun speaking, she poured herself a drink, saying in an undertone:

"I'm not offering you any. I don't want all that to start again."

"I don't want it anyway. Do you believe me now?"

"Do I believe what?"

"All I've been telling you."

And Sophie said almost regretfully:

"Yes."

"You can go on asking questions."

"You enjoy that, don't you?"

"I'm only anxious that there should be no more misapprehensions, that you should understand. I think you're beginning to understand. Throughout my life I've done everything one ought not to do, everything they tell us not to do."

She emphasized *they tell us.*

"I've paid for it, without complaining or asking for favors."

She skillfully corrected herself:

"Except from you."

"What favor have you asked from me?"

"You know very well. To let me make a nook for myself in your home."

"That's not true. You didn't know if I was alive or dead. It was I who came to get you from Rue de Jouy."

"I refused to go into a home. I threatened to jump out the window."

"You'd have done it."

"I would still do it."

It was not a threat. She uttered the words quietly, almost apologetically.

"However old one is, that's not an easy thing to do. But there comes a time when it seems preferable to anything else. Try to figure out, after what I've told you, how many years out of my fourscore I've really lived. You'd be surprised. When one puts together one's good moments, those when one has felt fully oneself, they amount to practically nothing, just a few memories one can count on one's fingers.

"And yet that's what one clings to.

"I regret nothing. I'm not even ashamed. I've no remorse. I've had no lack of time to think it over and try to understand.

"I shall remember things I've forgotten for the moment, which are probably important.

"I've wanted to get, and I've wanted to give. Not pity. I have never wanted pity and I've had none for other people. ..."

"I know!" Sophie blurted out.

And the old woman muttered, almost menacingly:

"No, you don't know. If you knew, you'd immediately send for ... what's his name?"

She rose, went toward the mantelpiece and read the card:

"Dr. Paul Barbanel ... Turbigo 47.94 ..."

Then, with a sudden change of tone:

"Let's have something to eat first. Aren't you hungry, too?"

EIGHT

When Lélia came in from the bedroom, a lock of hair hanging over her face and a shifty look in her eyes, it was obvious that a scene could not be avoided. She made an unconsciously ridiculous stage entrance, swaying her narrow hips and staring at the two women seated at the table, each in turn, with an air of would-be mockery which was merely aggressive.

Sophie said quietly:

"Sit down."

Lélia's lip curled. She was reluctant to jeopardize the security and comfort she enjoyed here, thanks to her friend. Yet she could not resist murmuring in a barely audible voice, like a child muttering threats but hoping they will not be heard:

"Do you think I should sit down?"

There was still time, and it was almost dramatic to watch her torn by conflicting impulses.

"Do you really want me to?"

One step farther and it would be too late to retreat. She took that step.

"Since you're back in the bosom of your family, I wonder . . ."

Lélia's voice took on a vulgar tone as she looked contemptuously at the old woman, who, in a cautious gesture of appeasement, laid her wrinkled hand on Sophie's.

"Sit down and shut up."

"I've still got the decency not to impose my presence when I feel I'm not wanted. Some people can't say as much."

The die was cast. No slap followed, because Sophie was sitting down and Lélia standing a few paces away, but Sophie's inexpressive gaze implied censure.

"Clear away her place, Louise."

Lélia mimicked her.

"Clear away her place, Louise! Let the girl go and eat somewhere else! Let the wretched creature find another hideout! We're full up here now. We've found our kind granny again and we've no further use for a loafer. I was expecting it, you know! One fine day it'll be her turn, then somebody else's."

She was pointing at Juliette.

"You'll come to realize that she's spiteful and that she hates you, that since she came into this house she's been doing her best to destroy you. Carry on, my girl! Defend yourself if you're equal to it. I won't be here to see which of the two wins the fight."

She went back into the bedroom and slammed the door so hard that the key fell out of the lock. It was only a false exit; her face reappeared almost immediately in the doorway.

"Enjoy your lunch!"

The door closed again, and they could hear her packing her things into suitcases. After a while she came back into the studio, without a glance at the two women sitting silently, to hunt through the piles of records and carry off those that belonged to her.

Juliette looked at Sophie, as though to say:

"Aren't you going to stop her from going?"

And Sophie, pretending not to understand, went on slowly eating. The maid went back and forth in silence. Outside, snow was falling. They heard Lélia telephoning to order a taxi. Then she made her final appearance, wearing a suit under her leopardskin coat and a fur hat on her pale hair.

She went up to Louise.

"I understand that in good society it's the custom, when one goes away, to leave a tip."

She held out some crumpled notes, and since Louise dared not take them, she let them drop on the carpet.

"Good luck to the three of you! Have a good time!"

She would have liked to have found a better exit line, but inspiration failed her, and soon afterward they heard her suitcases bumping against the walls in the hallway and the landing door was slammed.

There was a pause, a very long pause, and Juliette said at last, in a calm, toneless voice:

"There goes the cat's canary."

It was the time of day when the bars between the Champs-Elysées and the Seine, those bars with high stools that Sophie usually patronized, are all deserted. From its beginning the afternoon had taken on a peculiar color and rhythm, as though the girl had suddenly entered a nightmare world.

She had planned nothing. She had not gone out intending to drink, but, on the contrary, to clear her head by speeding along the main roads as she had thought of doing the day before.

At the wheel of her red car, she had crossed through the Bois de Boulogne and got as far as Saint-Cloud. But on reaching the highway she had been obliged to slow down and take her place in the long line of cars which moved with exasperating slowness because of the patches of frozen snow.

Two or three times she had tried to thread her way through the traffic, only to be stopped by a damaged car across the road, surrounded by gesticulating policemen, or by a stalled truck.

Eventually she had turned around and, on reaching Avenue George-V, had gone into the first bar, uneasy and dissatisfied.

"A Scotch, Jean."

She was sitting alone in front of the rows of bottles and the glasses decorated with little flags.

"You'll come to realize that she's spiteful and that she hates you. . . ."

Lélia, too, had found wounding words. She had not taught Sophie anything new, but now that the remark had been uttered, now that the words had made the idea more explicit, it was rather as though the thing itself had assumed a definitive form.

The Police Superintendent, in his anxiety to show himself a man of the world, had painted a picture of

156

the situation after his own fashion, a picture that was superficially accurate but, like certain paintings, too smooth, too harmonious, and his solution, which seemed so simple, had no real existence.

"The same again, Jean."

She would drink just enough to collect her wits and to acquire some degree of inner warmth; then she would stop.

Juliette had answered her questions and wanted nothing better than to go on answering them, with complacent exhibitionism. As she had been careful to stress, she talked only about herself, discussed only her own case, accused nobody.

And yet what emerged from her confession was more depressing than an indictment.

Sophie tried to pull herself together, to recover some degree of poise. The barman, elbows on the counter, tried to engage her in friendly conversation, but because she had no desire to talk to him or to listen to him she preferred to leave and seek shelter in another bar, on Rue François-Ier.

Here there was only one couple, at the far end, and they would probably slip, by and by, into the nearest available hotel. The woman would undress in the drab room, and they would make love, crudely, as in an obscene photograph.

Juliette . . .

She wanted to think about something else, and yet her thoughts reverted invariably to her grandmother, to words and scraps of phrases and ideas that had been flung out and implanted in her and that were becoming increasingly pregnant with meaning.

A few days earlier Sophie had felt unattached, rootless, as if she were without a family, and now she found herself linked to the dead, to figures who watched her as though they had rights over her, as though they had some say as to her future fate.

Even her father, the only person whom she could remember light-heartedly, almost without bitterness, seemed now to belong to the old woman, who had enticed him into her camp. There had been affinities between them—Juliette had spoken the truth there—furtive contacts, chocolate and buns laid in secret on the corner of a chest.

God knows how, with a few words the old woman had created an unreal picture which nonetheless took shape in the girl's mind: her father and a younger Juliette smiling at one another, hand in hand, ecstatic, the Juliette of old who had made men want to ask her what she thought of them.

For two or three hours at a stretch, sometimes plunging into the cold air and the snow, which now fell more densely, and then hoisting herself onto a high stool, pointing to a bottle of Scotch, lighting a cigarette with an ever shakier hand, she struggled to escape from her grandmother, and succeeded only in sinking ever deeper into the old woman's world.

Hadn't her grandmother been playing this game all her life? She had become expert at it, and every thrust told. Some of these were so subtle that one didn't feel them at the time, but only when, later on, the wound started to fester.

It all seemed true, it was all true, an ice-cold, cruel, unrelenting truth.

The old woman had not bothered to ask any questions, to reveal her curiosity. Because she knew it all! She had almost never talked about Sophie. She had not judged her. But she had forced her to judge herself.

"Isn't Lélia with you?"

Darkness had fallen. Shadowy figures had begun to haunt the bars, which gradually filled with voices and smoke. Seeking peace among anonymous companions, Sophie, who lacked the heart to go home, crossed the Champs-Elysées and went down Rue du Colisée.

Here the crowd was different and so were the bars. Whenever she failed to find Scotch, she would leave the place, followed by mocking glances.

When Lélia had made her embarrassing entry and exit, the old woman had uttered only a single sentence, brief and final as an epitaph. She had been quite right. She was always quite right. In any event Lélia would have left one day or another. And it was probably true, too, that she would not live to be old.

Juliette had a genius for putting her finger on people's weak points, on wounds that one thought had healed. She would touch them gently, without pressure, as though in a caress, and it hurt, with a pain that did not disappear but, on the contrary, spread.

Sophie was half tipsy; she was aware of it, she could see it when she caught a glimpse of her face in a mirror between two bottles. It was too late to stop, and perhaps it was better so. Maybe she would not go back to Quai de Bourbon tonight but would sleep somewhere else, no matter where, if only for the sake of infuriating the old woman who was waiting and watching.

The most exasperating thing was that she had nothing to reproach her for. Wasn't it natural that at the age of eighty, having found a member of her family again, she should feel the need to unburden herself, and hadn't Sophie herself encouraged her to do so?

It was hard to explain. On Juliette's lips, words and even people's names became oppressive and threatening. The figures that her story evoked assumed the implacable immobility of statues.

At the same time, without one's being conscious of it, she would utter other words, kindly words, such as usually prove reassuring, and from being uttered by her they were emptied of their beneficence.

Sophie, too, had been doing her utmost for years. No! She could not and would not say that or even think it, since that other woman had declared:

"You and I, we're too much alike. . . ."

As though both of them bore some terrifying stigmata!

In her struggle, she was aware of animated faces, lips and eyes, cheeks reddened by the chill of the streets; she breathed the odor of various apéritifs, and of coffee; words and sentences were being uttered around her, and men were nudging one another as they pointed to her.

She shrugged her shoulders. All this, and the pedestrians hurrying along the sidewalks, the passengers sitting motionless in the cold light of buses, the beggar with his snow-covered beard, the shop windows, the dark corners—all this teeming life belonged to a world from which she was separated by an invisible world. Was it even real?

Juliette had been quite right. What was it that she had said? One ought to have noted down each of her remarks, to avoid imprecision. Everything counts, particularly shades of meaning, and where her grandmother was concerned there were so many shades of meaning.

Had she not spent eighty years thinking? A little machine nibbling away, under a skull now covered only by a transparent veil of hair.

"... I tried to cling to ..."

No! There was something else, something more important, that had to be recovered, because it had been said for Sophie's special benefit.

"... I tried to take ..."

To take something from men, to extract strength and serenity from them.

"... Then I tried to give ..."

Had she not claimed that this was ultimately the same thing, the same symptom of weakness? One takes because one is weak. One gives in order to convince oneself that one is strong, which is just another sign of weakness.

It was as wearisome as a walk by night along the ruts of a farm lane.

Was it to Adrien that she had sought to give something, the second time she had lived with him?

Sophie had barely caught sight of him in the darkness of Boulevard Saint-Germain. To her, for years, he had been only a figure remembered from childhood and known as "the tramp."

Now he had become Adrien, and his armchair was part of the furniture on Quai de Bourbon.

Her grandfather was Prédicant, without a Christian

161

name, and strangely enough this seemed quite natural to Sophie.

A man was looking at her with gleaming eyes, a young Spaniard in a leather jacket, with callused hands, and there was arrogance as well as timidity in his attitude.

A short while back, on Rue François-Ier, she had imagined a room, a bed, a couple, and just because her picture had the same anatomical accuracy as Juliette's stories, she was suddenly tempted. Wasn't this a way of escape, if only for a brief moment?

She did not avert her head, but stared back at the unknown face, whose lips were curled in a conceited smile under a short mustache.

The waiter was watching them from behind his counter. She asked for her check.

The Spaniard had mimed a question. She had replied by a flicker of her eyelids, and when she had gone ten yards down the street, she heard hurrying footsteps behind her.

Juliette had asked to be allowed to feel the mink lining of her raincoat. The Spaniard, however, did not bother to do so, being just as sure that it was rabbit as he was mistaken about his companion.

She had to choose the hotel, since he did not know the district. He could hardly get over such a stroke of luck, but he was puzzled by the girl's not asking for money in advance and by the way she stripped naked without saying a word, before even drawing the curtains.

When he left, she did not follow him, and the chambermaid, coming in soon after with clean towels, found her deeply asleep.

Sophie woke without being aware that it was very late at night, heard buses pass close to the windows, realized that she was not at home on the Ile Saint-Louis, and felt for a light switch. The bedcovers, the armchair, the tablecloth were of dubious cleanliness.

When she went downstairs, the night porter ran after her.

"It's fifteen francs. I'll have to charge you for the night."

She paid in a dream and went to look for her car, having forgotten where she had parked it. She went into a couple more bars before reaching Avenue George-V.

"She hates me," she muttered mindlessly, like an incantation. What matter if it was Lélia who had told her that? Was Lélia at La Patate now, singing, or drinking by herself in her corner?

It was decidedly a day for getting drunk—for Lélia as much as for her. They had nothing better to do. The old woman had won. She would always win. It was impossible to kill her, just as Juliette herself hadn't dared to kill Prédicant because it was too dangerous.

Sophie, driving her car, felt proud of seeing the red light in time and stopping short. It seemed to her that the policeman on duty was looking at her with a suspicious eye. She had done nothing wrong. She had stopped. She was waiting for the green light, to start off again, and it wasn't her fault if her car jerked excitedly forward. A taste of garlic reminded her of the Spaniard, whom she would never see again and who had taken her for a drunken tart.

She had looked at him straight. She had even

163

looked at him the whole time, while thinking about things her grandmother had said.

She mustn't end by pitying herself. Juliette did not ask for pity. Juliette had no pity. What was it that she'd said?

"... No, you don't know. If you knew, you'd immediately send for Dr. Barbanel."

The Police Superintendent, who was so polite, had taken the trouble to call on Sophie to offer her that solution. Why shouldn't it be the right one? What was it that the old woman had not yet confessed. Something dreadful enough to make one want to shut her up immediately?

"I'm drunk and I hate her."

Furiously, she switched off the engine, leaped out of the car, and slammed the door as violently as Lélia had closed that of the bedroom. She was being deliberately noisy because she was at home, at Sophie Emel's home, the real Sophie Emel, who had worked hard to become what she was, not the Sophie that her grandmother was trying to create.

Nobody had the right! She turned on lights everywhere, and without taking off her coat or her shoes went through the kitchen, resolutely, straight toward the door behind which she knew the old woman was not asleep.

She must have slept, however, for her face, suddenly revealed by the ceiling light, was once again limp and puffy, with flushed cheekbones and red-rimmed eyes. She was drunk! Two empty bottles standing on the table beside a dirty glass, looking like a still life, bore witness to the fact.

They were both drunk, equally drunk. Tonight everybody was drunk, and it was a good opportunity to have things out.

The old woman was frightened and kept silent while Sophie, with an air of deliberation, went to fetch some whisky from the studio and returned.

"Do you want some, too?"

"No, thanks. I've already drunk too much."

"And when you've been drinking do you feel any pity?"

Juliette's eyes revealed terror.

"What do you mean? Pity for whom? Are you talking about Lélia?"

She was not so perspicacious after all, since her mind was still on Lélia, whereas Lélia had been out of the picture for a long time. Lélia was probably drunk, too, at this moment.

"Pity for yourself! You told me . . ."

"What did I tell you?"

"You told me . . . Now listen! . . . You told me that you had no pity for other people, and that if I knew . . ."

Juliette pulled the bedclothes up to her chin as though in self-protection.

"Do you remember?"

"I think so."

"It was before lunch. . . . That I would send for Dr. Barbanel . . ."

"Do you want to send for him?"

"No! What I want is to know just how cruel you are. For you are cruel, aren't you?"

"I'm unhappy, Sophie."

"It's possible to be unhappy and cruel at the same time. Tell me!"

"Tell you what, for heaven's sake?"

"You know very well. I can see it in your eyes. I'm drunk, I know, but I'm clearheaded."

She repeated, pleased with having found the words:

"Drunk, but clearheaded."

"Sophie!"

"Go on."

"Are you anxious to get rid of me? Do you want me to go away?"

"I want you to tell the truth."

"What truth?"

She was still trying to dodge the issue with her questions.

"You know very well that I've told you the truth."

"Not the whole truth."

"What makes you think that?"

"You do."

"Don't drink any more, Sophie. You can't see the state you're in. I'm sick. I feel bad. You'd better fetch Louise to look after me."

"If you're sick, I shall send for Dr. Barbanel."

"For pity's sake!"

"Tell me."

Realizing that there was no way of escape, Juliette resigned herself.

"It was about Adrien. It doesn't concern you, because you didn't know him and he means nothing to you."

"What did you do to Adrien?"

"It wasn't me. It was Adrien himself. I'm very old, Sophie, an old woman with not much longer to live, and you stand there threatening me."

"Adrien?"

"He'd been a helpless invalid for months, bedridden and incontinent. And yet I had to go and fetch him drink. He demanded it; he became more and more demanding. And when his pains began he would groan so loud that the neighbors started banging on the walls. He was bad-tempered. He called me the old woman and he seemed to hold me responsible. I was exhausted from going up and down five flights of stairs to fetch all the things he demanded."

Sophie stood swaying, clutching her bottle, ready to take another swig.

"He would never consent to see a doctor. He was frightened. He knew they'd have taken him to a hospital, and that he'd never have come out again."

"Did you kill him?"

The old woman suddenly turned pale.

"Why do you say that?"

"Because I insist on hearing the truth."

"It wasn't me. It was himself, I tell you. When he was in too much pain, he would take some pills—I don't even know what they were. In the bistros of the Saint-Paul district, when he was still able to crawl there, he'd got to know a former pharmacist, who'd had to give it all up because he drank. They called him Doc. He had a habit of handing out medicine that he pulled out of his pockets and that he'd kept from the days when he had a dispensary. I knew where to find him when we ran out of pills. 'One at a time,' he would tell me with a queer sort of laugh. 'Never more than two.' I swear to you I still don't know what they were. Then one day Adrien took two. He was drunk. He was screaming with pain. The pills quieted him, and he dozed off for a moment.

"When he was in that state, he didn't know where he was, or the time, or anything else, and sometimes he'd wake me up in the middle of the night thinking it was morning."

"Were you sorry for him?"

"What do you mean? Stop drinking, I implore you. I'll do whatever you like, but you mustn't go on looking at me like that. I'll go away tomorrow morning, if you tell me to, at daybreak, but put down that bottle and stop looking so fierce."

"What did you do exactly?"

"I didn't have the strength to go on. It was no sort of life, either for him or for me. After about ten minutes or a quarter of an hour, he woke up, looked at the bedside table and asked:

" 'Why don't you give me my pills? Do you want me to die?'

"That's what he said. It's the truth."

"Did you give them to him?"

"He insisted."

"Did he die immediately?"

"Five hours afterward."

"Did you have to give the pills a third time?"

Sophie, unaware of the expression on her face, was staring with disgust at the old woman, who, in her nightgown, had slid out of bed and was kneeling at her feet.

"Forgive me, Sophie? You didn't let me explain. You asked me such harsh questions. It wasn't like that."

Sophie repulsed her, and drank from the mouth of the bottle as if she wanted to knock herself out.

Adrien was unimportant. What the old woman had done was unimportant. Now it was just between the two of them that something was taking place, something that was beyond their control.

"Clearheaded!" She laughed derisively.

"What did you say?"

"Nothing."

"Sophie!"

But Sophie, freeing her legs from the old woman's clutch, left the room, went into her own, locked the door, and flung herself down fully dressed upon the bed.

Her teeth clenched, she abandoned herself to her nightmare, putting up no resistance as it engulfed her, but, on the contrary, feeling a kind of pleasure in sinking ever deeper.

No pity! It was all so true that it became false. There was no more truth, no more tears or smiles, nothing but statues *devoid of pity!*

"Sophie!"

The old woman was screaming somewhere, but the thought of replying never occurred to her. It was all, already, in the past.

"Sophie, I beg you, let me in! I need to see you, to feel you near me. I need to have you say something to me. I'm old, I'm sick. I won't hurt you any more, I promise. I'll keep silent. I . . . ."

She was banging on the door with her fists, and the sound echoed as though in another world.

"Sophie, if you don't open the door, I'm going to . . ."

For a moment Sophie raised her head from her pillow to listen.

"If you don't open the door, if you don't say you forgive me, I shall do what I said I would, and you won't see me again. . . ."

The girl let her head fall back, relapsed into the teeming gloom of her nightmare, and eventually fell asleep, with a grim look on her face.

Through her sleep, she became aware of the muffled sound of knocking, and a different voice, that of Louise, calling:

"Mademoiselle, it's the police!"

She could not understand how that concerned her. Then another voice asked:

"Haven't you got a second key?"

"I think the key of my room fits the lock."

And then the maid was shaking her by the shoulder and putting a glass of cold water to her lips.

"Your grandmother . . ."

"What?"

A young policeman, whose rosy cheeks were cold from the night air, was standing in the doorway muttering in some embarrassment:

"I'd like you to come down to identify the body that my partner and I have just found on the sidewalk. . . ."

It was night outside. The concierge, in her dressing gown, with her hair in curlers, was watching impassively from behind the glass door of her lodge. Four or five people were standing around in the newly fallen snow, where footsteps marked trails.

"The concierge says that this is somebody who lives in your home. Is that so?"

"It's my grandmother."

The two policemen stared at one another, then stared again at the dazed-looking girl, who smelled of drink and who was still fully dressed from the night before, down to her shoes and her fur-lined raincoat.

"The Superintendent will probably come up and see you soon."

She climbed the five flights, occasionally bumping into the wall.

Louise was waiting for her, with a stern, tragic look.

"You can be grateful to me for not telling anything."

And since Sophie seemed not to hear:

"When I think that you went and woke up that poor old woman in the middle of the night to torture her! I won't leave today, so as not to injure your reputation. But as soon as the formalities are over . . ."

Dr. Barbanel's card was still on the marble mantelpiece, and Sophie mechanically tore it to shreds.

Then she sat down, alone at last in the studio, where someone, the policeman or Louise, had closed the window again, and she waited for the Superintendent, who must have been getting dressed.

Her glance happened to fall on the clock, and she was surprised to see that it was only four in the morning. There must still be a few guests left, and music, at La Patate.

She was going to have to begin all over again, to find something else to fasten on to.

Wasn't it Juliette who had said that?

Forever Juliette!

Noland, January 13, 1959